Archie

– in –

Snooze Button

COPPER CANYON
ELEMENTARY

visit us at
www.abdopublishing.com

Exclusive Spotlight library bound edition published in 2007 by Spotlight, a division of ABDO Publishing Group, Edina, Minnesota. Spotlight produces high quality reinforced library bound editions for schools and libraries. Published by agreement with Archie Comic Publications, Inc.

Library of Congress Cataloging-in-Publication Data

Archie in Snooze button / edited by Nelson Ribeiro & Victor Gorelick.
    p. cm. -- (The Archie digest library)
    Revision of issue no. 179 (May 2001) of Archie digest magazine.
    ISBN-13: 978-1-59961-261-4
    ISBN-10: 1-59961-261-5
    1. Comic books, strips, etc. I. Ribeiro, Nelson. II. Gorelick, Victor. III. Archie digest magazine. 179. IV. Title: Snooze button.

PN6728.A72A73 2007
741.5'973--dc22

2006049179

All Spotlight books are reinforced library binding and manufactured in the United States of America.

Contents

Archie®

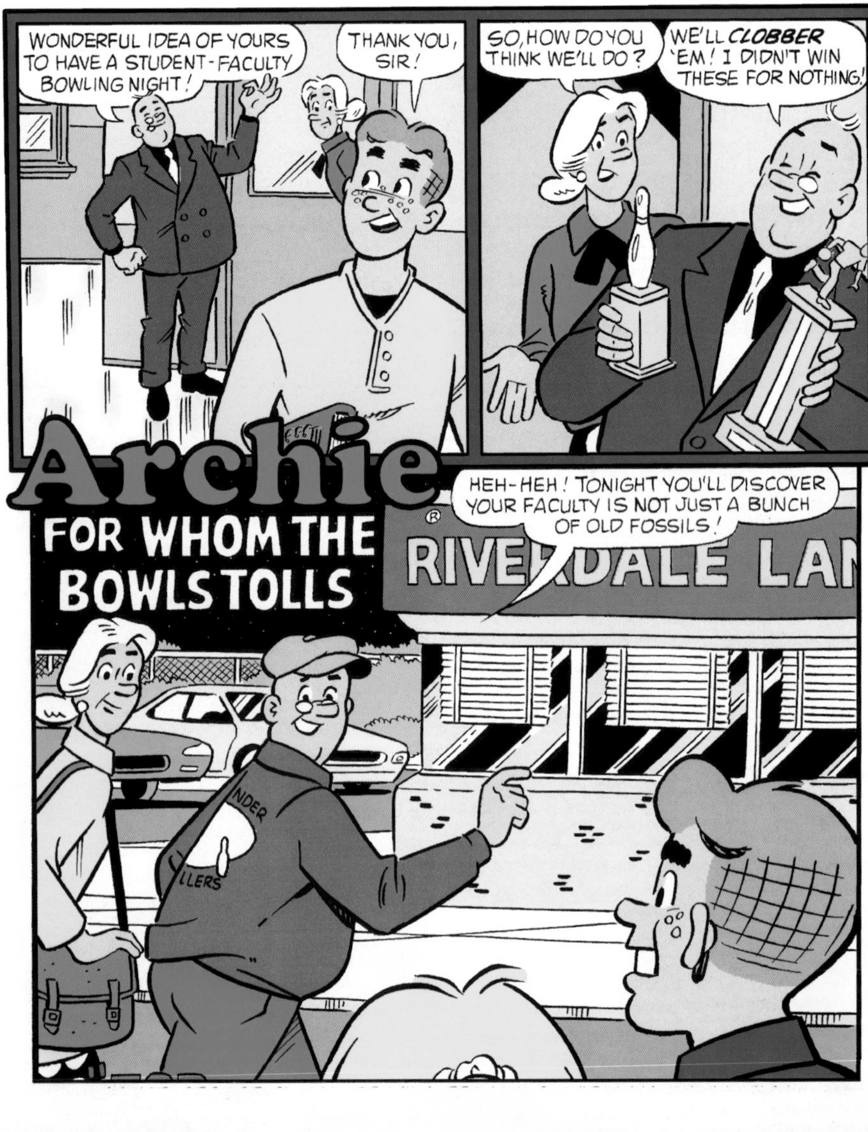
WONDERFUL IDEA OF YOURS TO HAVE A STUDENT-FACULTY BOWLING NIGHT!
THANK YOU, SIR!
SO, HOW DO YOU THINK WE'LL DO?
WE'LL CLOBBER 'EM! I DIDN'T WIN THESE FOR NOTHING!
Archie®
FOR WHOM THE BOWLS TOLLS
HEH-HEH! TONIGHT YOU'LL DISCOVER YOUR FACULTY IS NOT JUST A BUNCH OF OLD FOSSILS!
RIVERDALE LAN
INDER
LLERS

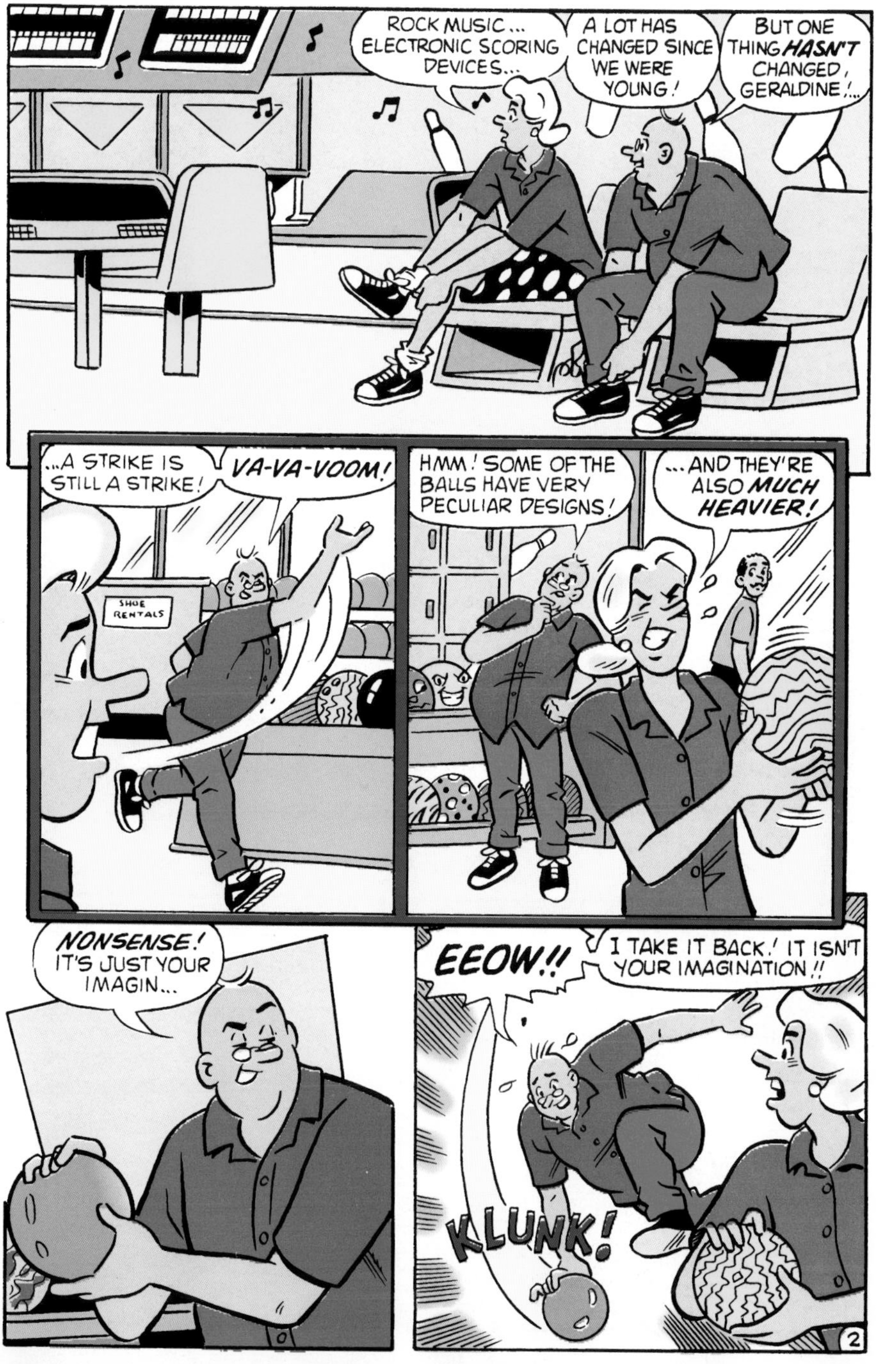
ROCK MUSIC... ELECTRONIC SCORING DEVICES...
A LOT HAS CHANGED SINCE WE WERE YOUNG!
BUT ONE THING HASN'T CHANGED, GERALDINE!...
...A STRIKE IS STILL A STRIKE!
VA-VA-VOOM!
SHOE RENTALS
HMM! SOME OF THE BALLS HAVE VERY PECULIAR DESIGNS!
...AND THEY'RE ALSO MUCH HEAVIER!
NONSENSE! IT'S JUST YOUR IMAGIN...
EEOW!!
I TAKE IT BACK! IT ISN'T YOUR IMAGINATION!!
KLUNK!
2

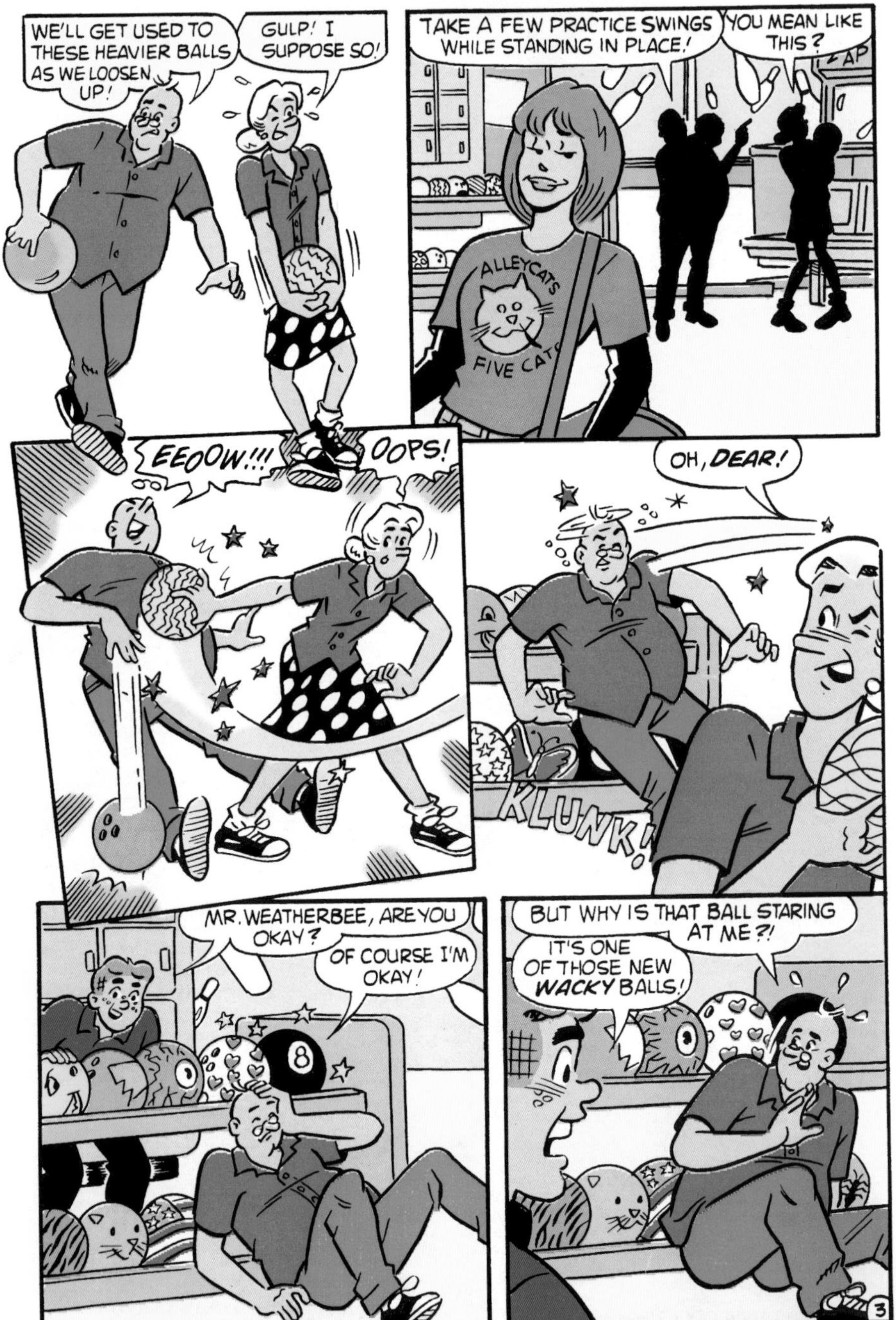
WE'LL GET USED TO THESE HEAVIER BALLS AS WE LOOSEN UP!
GULP! I SUPPOSE SO!
TAKE A FEW PRACTICE SWINGS WHILE STANDING IN PLACE!
YOU MEAN LIKE THIS?
ALLEYCATS
FIVE CATS
EEOOW!!!
OOPS!
OH, DEAR!
KLUNK!
MR. WEATHERBEE, ARE YOU OKAY?
OF COURSE I'M OKAY!
BUT WHY IS THAT BALL STARING AT ME?!
IT'S ONE OF THOSE NEW WACKY BALLS!
3

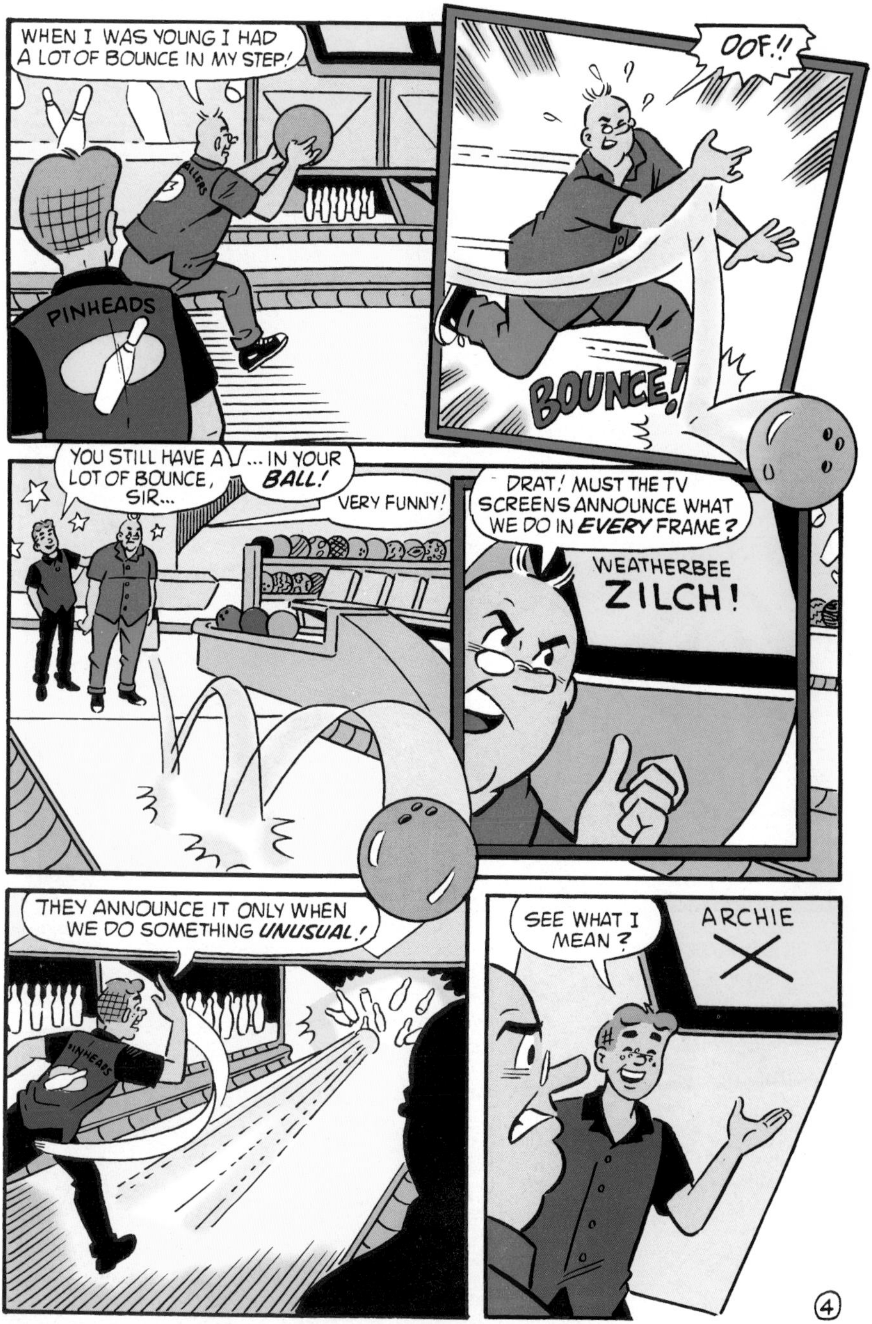
WHEN I WAS YOUNG I HAD A LOT OF BOUNCE IN MY STEP!
BALLERS
PINHEADS
OOF!!
BOUNCE!
YOU STILL HAVE A LOT OF BOUNCE, SIR...
... IN YOUR BALL!
VERY FUNNY!
DRAT! MUST THE TV SCREENS ANNOUNCE WHAT WE DO IN EVERY FRAME?
WEATHERBEE
ZILCH!
THEY ANNOUNCE IT ONLY WHEN WE DO SOMETHING UNUSUAL!
PINHEADS
SEE WHAT I MEAN?
ARCHIE
4

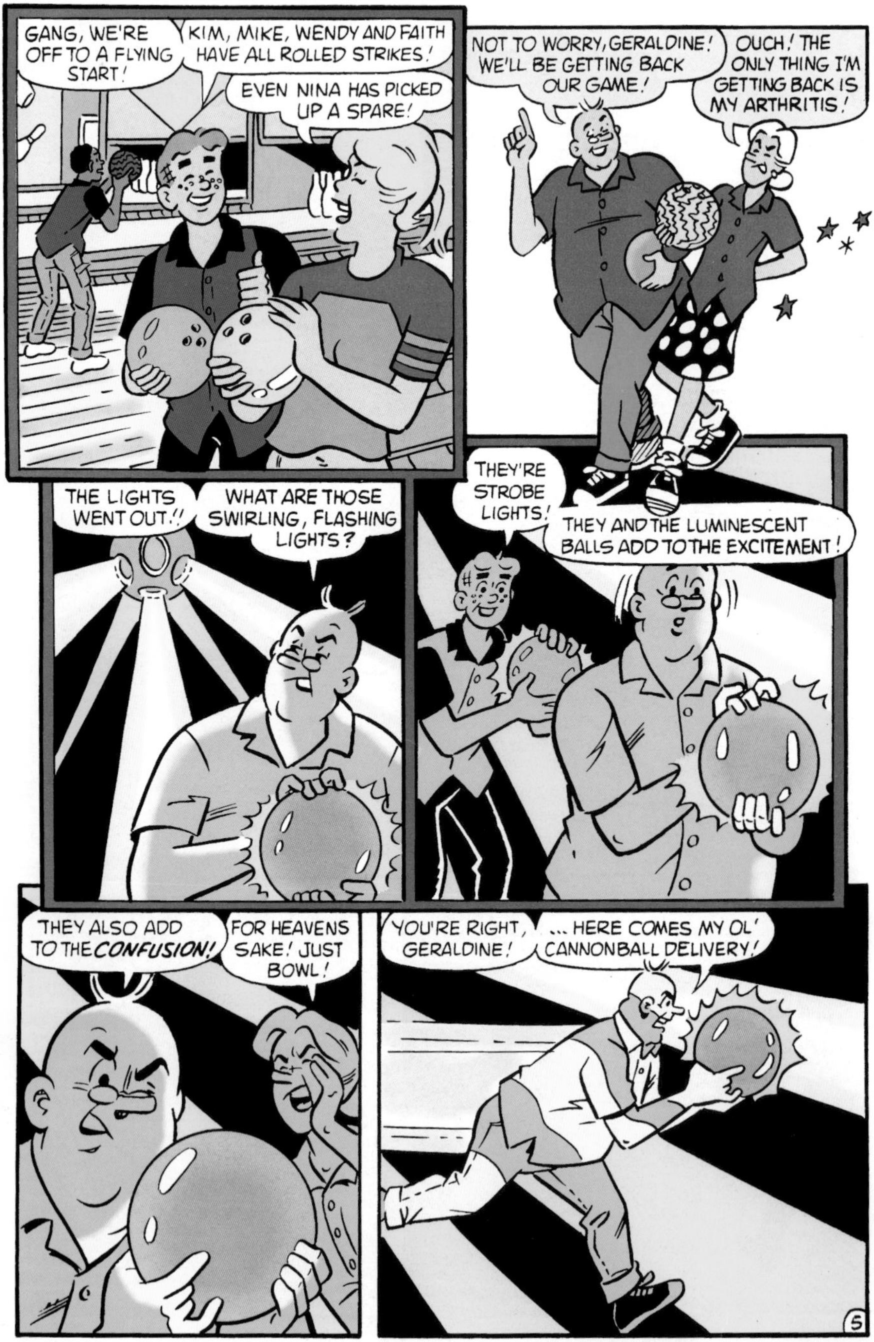
GANG, WE'RE OFF TO A FLYING START!
KIM, MIKE, WENDY AND FAITH HAVE ALL ROLLED STRIKES!
EVEN NINA HAS PICKED UP A SPARE!
NOT TO WORRY, GERALDINE! WE'LL BE GETTING BACK OUR GAME!
OUCH! THE ONLY THING I'M GETTING BACK IS MY ARTHRITIS!
THE LIGHTS WENT OUT!!
WHAT ARE THOSE SWIRLING, FLASHING LIGHTS?
THEY'RE STROBE LIGHTS!
THEY AND THE LUMINESCENT BALLS ADD TO THE EXCITEMENT!
THEY ALSO ADD TO THE CONFUSION!
FOR HEAVENS SAKE! JUST BOWL!
YOU'RE RIGHT, GERALDINE!
... HERE COMES MY OL' CANNONBALL DELIVERY!
5

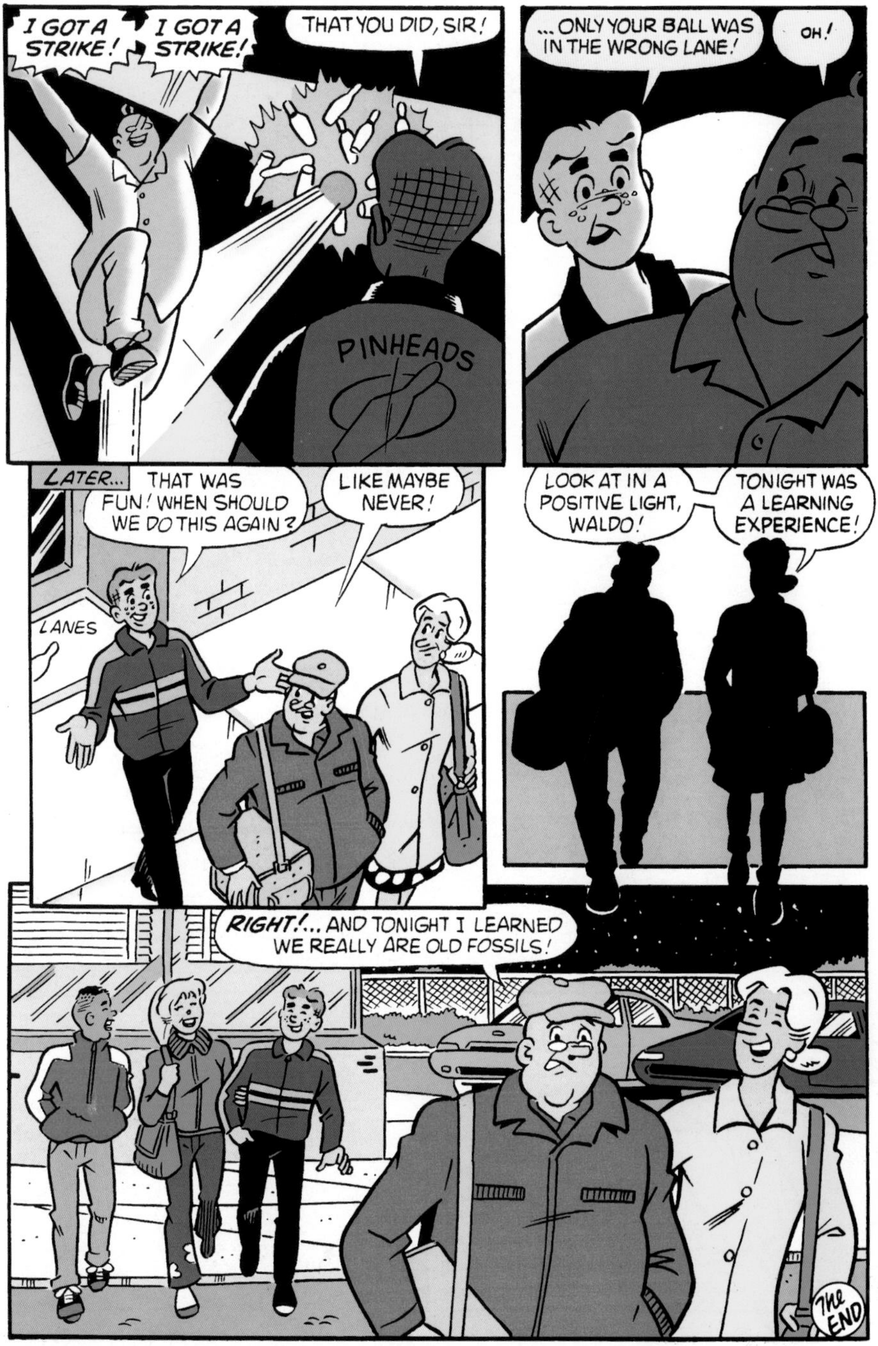
I GOT A STRIKE!
I GOT A STRIKE!
THAT YOU DID, SIR!
PINHEADS
... ONLY YOUR BALL WAS IN THE WRONG LANE!
OH!
LATER...
THAT WAS FUN! WHEN SHOULD WE DO THIS AGAIN?
LIKE MAYBE NEVER!
LANES
LOOK AT IN A POSITIVE LIGHT, WALDO!
TONIGHT WAS A LEARNING EXPERIENCE!
RIGHT!... AND TONIGHT I LEARNED WE REALLY ARE OLD FOSSILS!
THE END

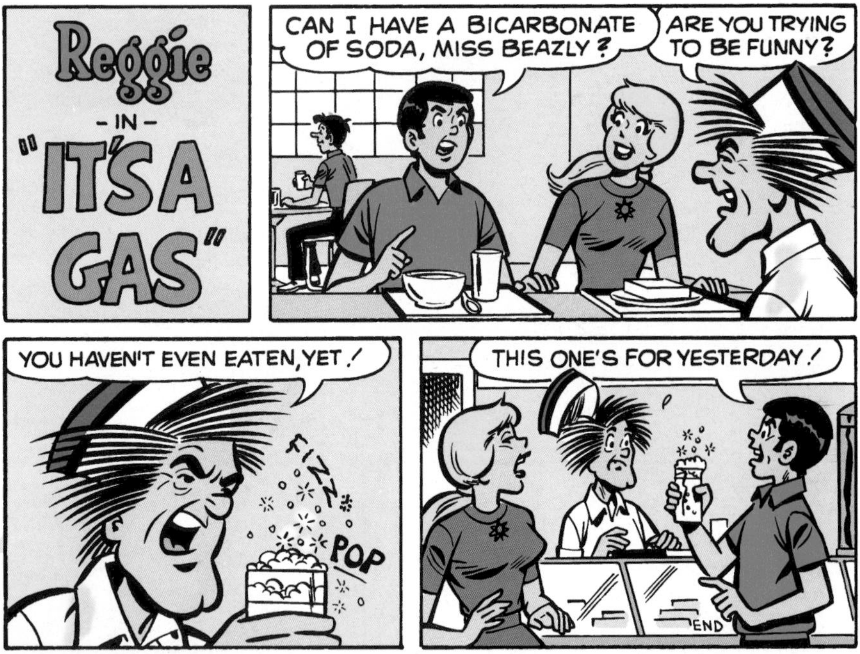
Reggie
-IN-
"IT'S A GAS"
CAN I HAVE A BICARBONATE OF SODA, MISS BEAZLY?
ARE YOU TRYING TO BE FUNNY?
YOU HAVEN'T EVEN EATEN, YET!
FIZZ
POP
THIS ONE'S FOR YESTERDAY!
END

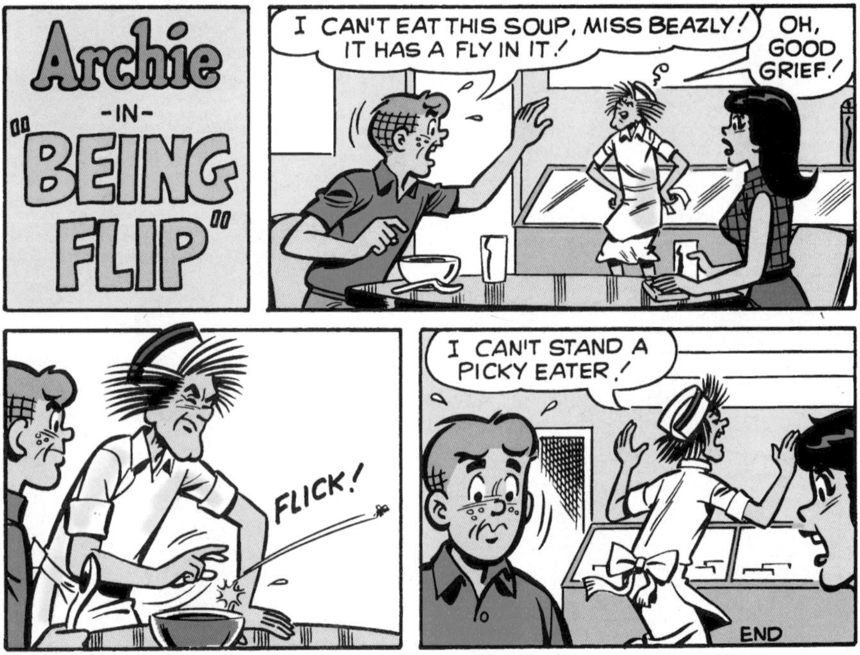
Archie
-IN-
"BEING FLIP"
I CAN'T EAT THIS SOUP, MISS BEAZLY! IT HAS A FLY IN IT!
OH, GOOD GRIEF!
FLICK!
I CAN'T STAND A PICKY EATER!
END

Moose GAG BAG

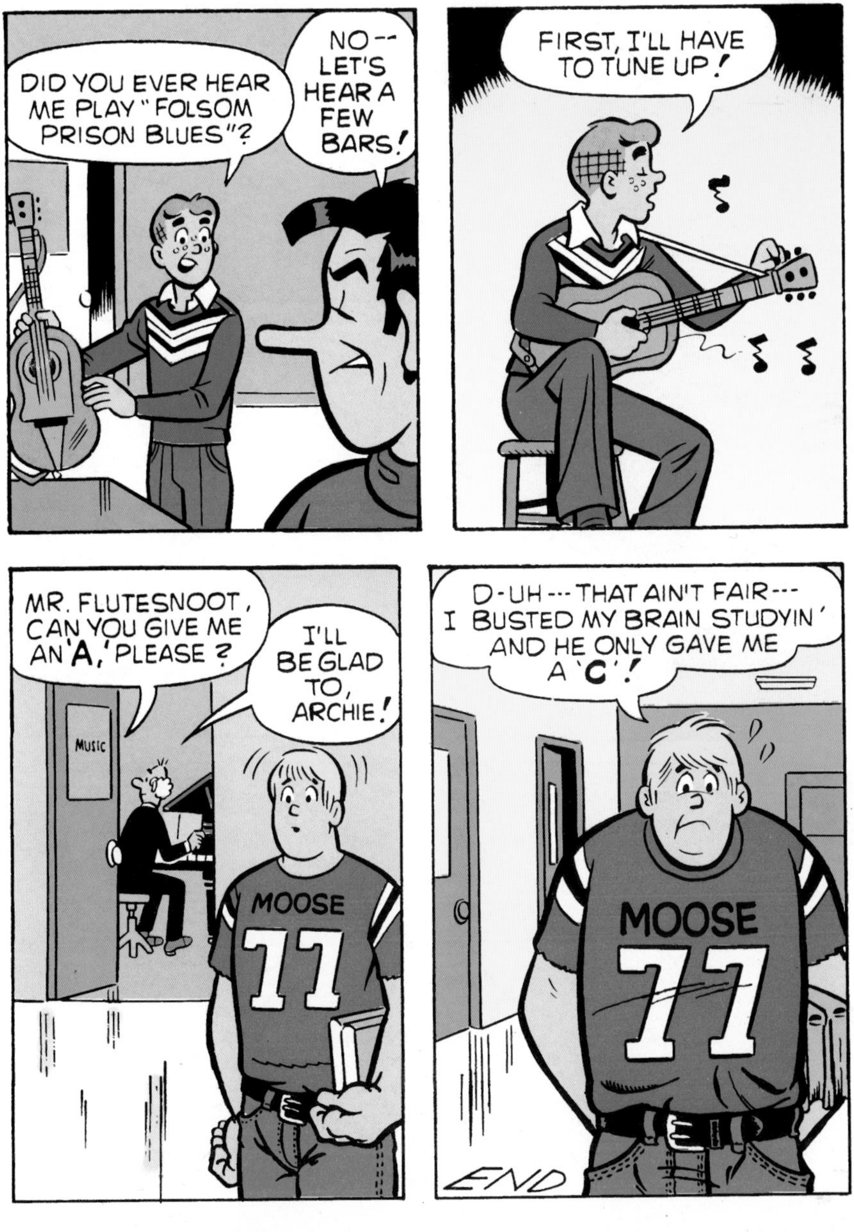
DID YOU EVER HEAR ME PLAY "FOLSOM PRISON BLUES"?
NO -- LET'S HEAR A FEW BARS!
FIRST, I'LL HAVE TO TUNE UP!
MR. FLUTESNOOT, CAN YOU GIVE ME AN 'A,' PLEASE?
I'LL BE GLAD TO, ARCHIE!
MUSIC
MOOSE 77
D-UH --- THAT AIN'T FAIR --- I BUSTED MY BRAIN STUDYIN' AND HE ONLY GAVE ME A 'C'!
MOOSE 77
END

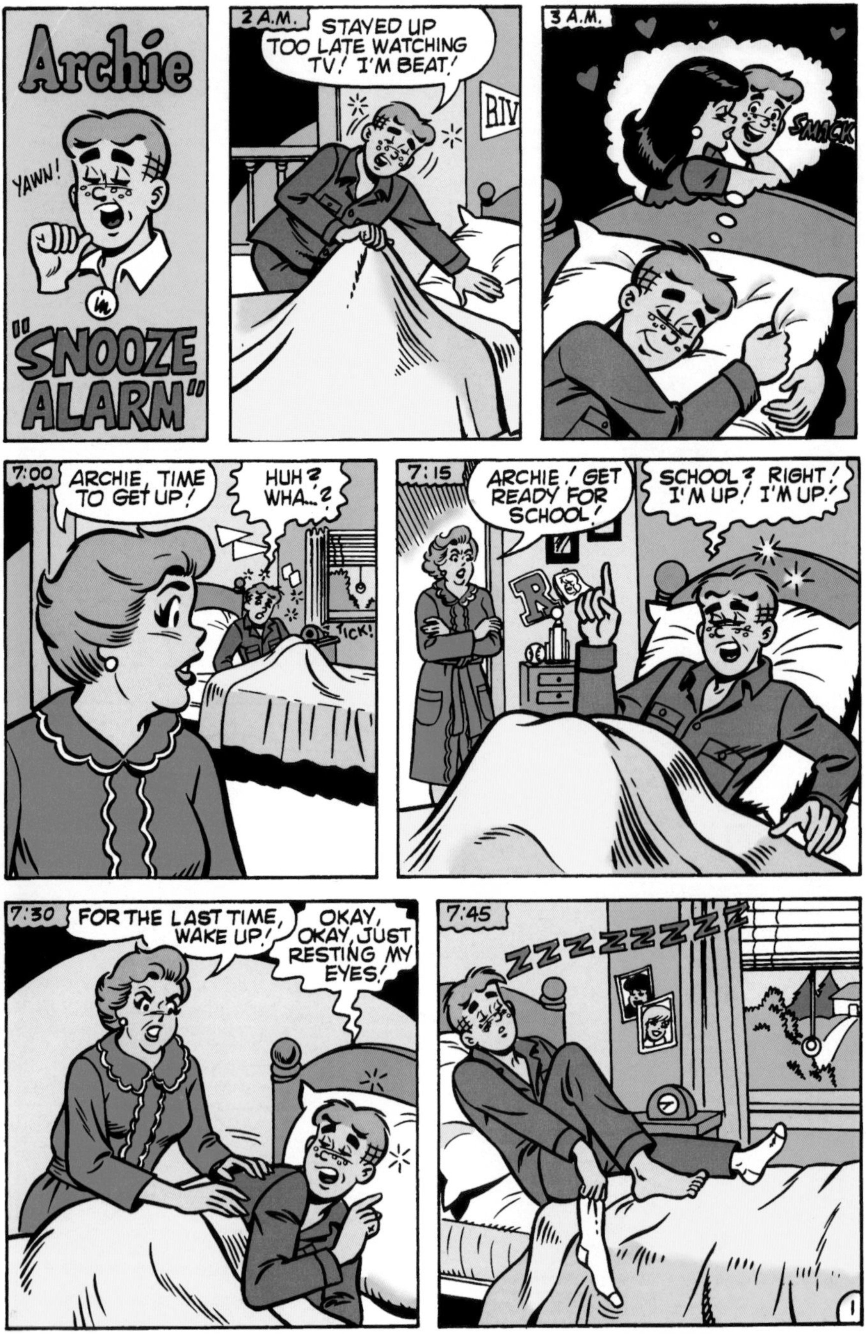
Archie
YAWN!
"SNOOZE ALARM"
2 A.M.
STAYED UP TOO LATE WATCHING TV! I'M BEAT!
3 A.M.
SMACK
7:00
ARCHIE, TIME TO GET UP!
HUH? WHA...?
TICK!
7:15
ARCHIE! GET READY FOR SCHOOL!
SCHOOL? RIGHT! I'M UP! I'M UP!
7:30
FOR THE LAST TIME, WAKE UP!
OKAY, OKAY, JUST RESTING MY EYES!
7:45
ZZZZZZZZZ
1

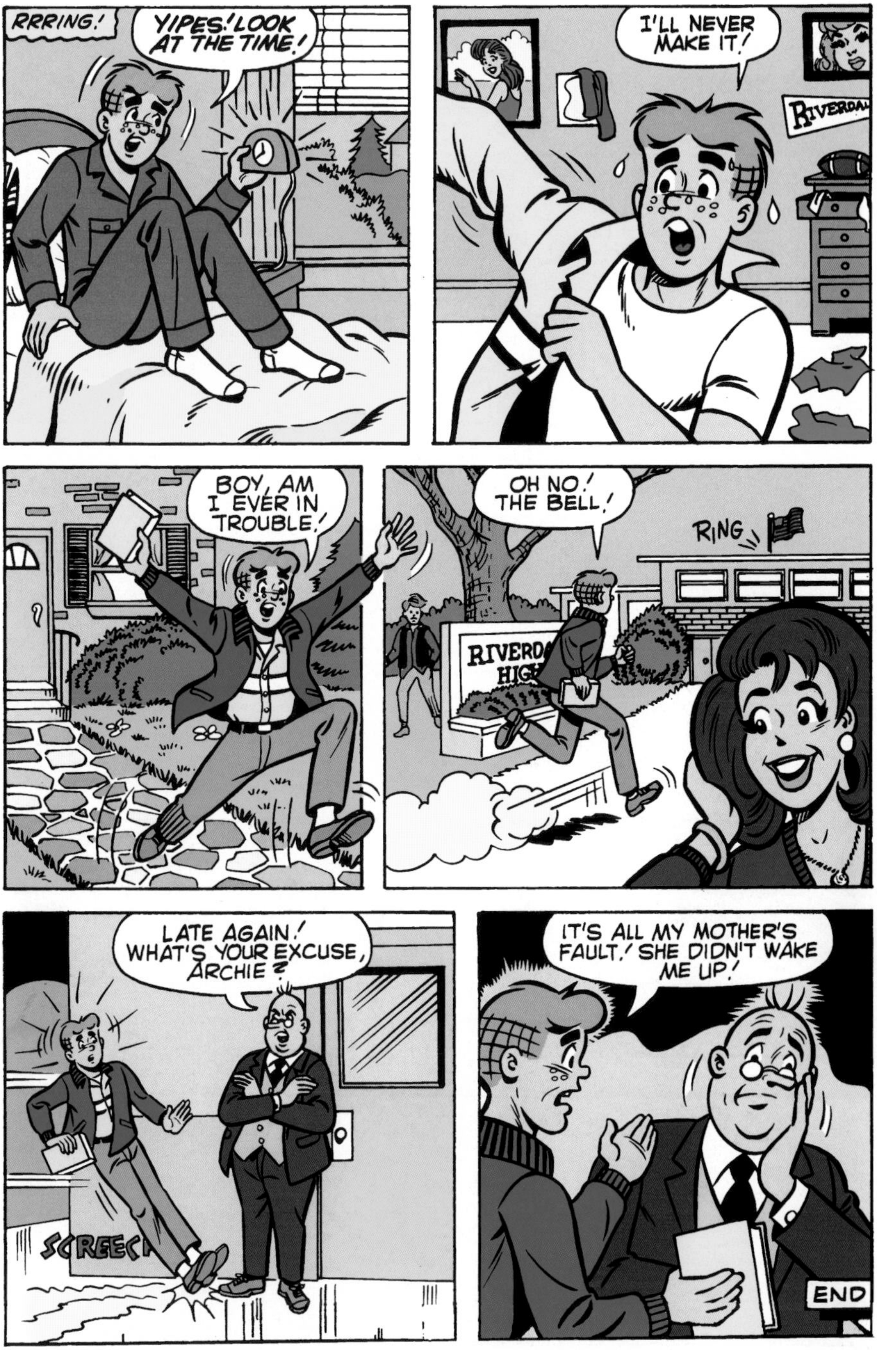
RRRING!
YIPES! LOOK AT THE TIME!
I'LL NEVER MAKE IT!
RIVERDA
BOY, AM I EVER IN TROUBLE!
OH NO! THE BELL!
RING
RIVERDA HIGH
LATE AGAIN! WHAT'S YOUR EXCUSE, ARCHIE?
SCREECH
IT'S ALL MY MOTHER'S FAULT! SHE DIDN'T WAKE ME UP!
END

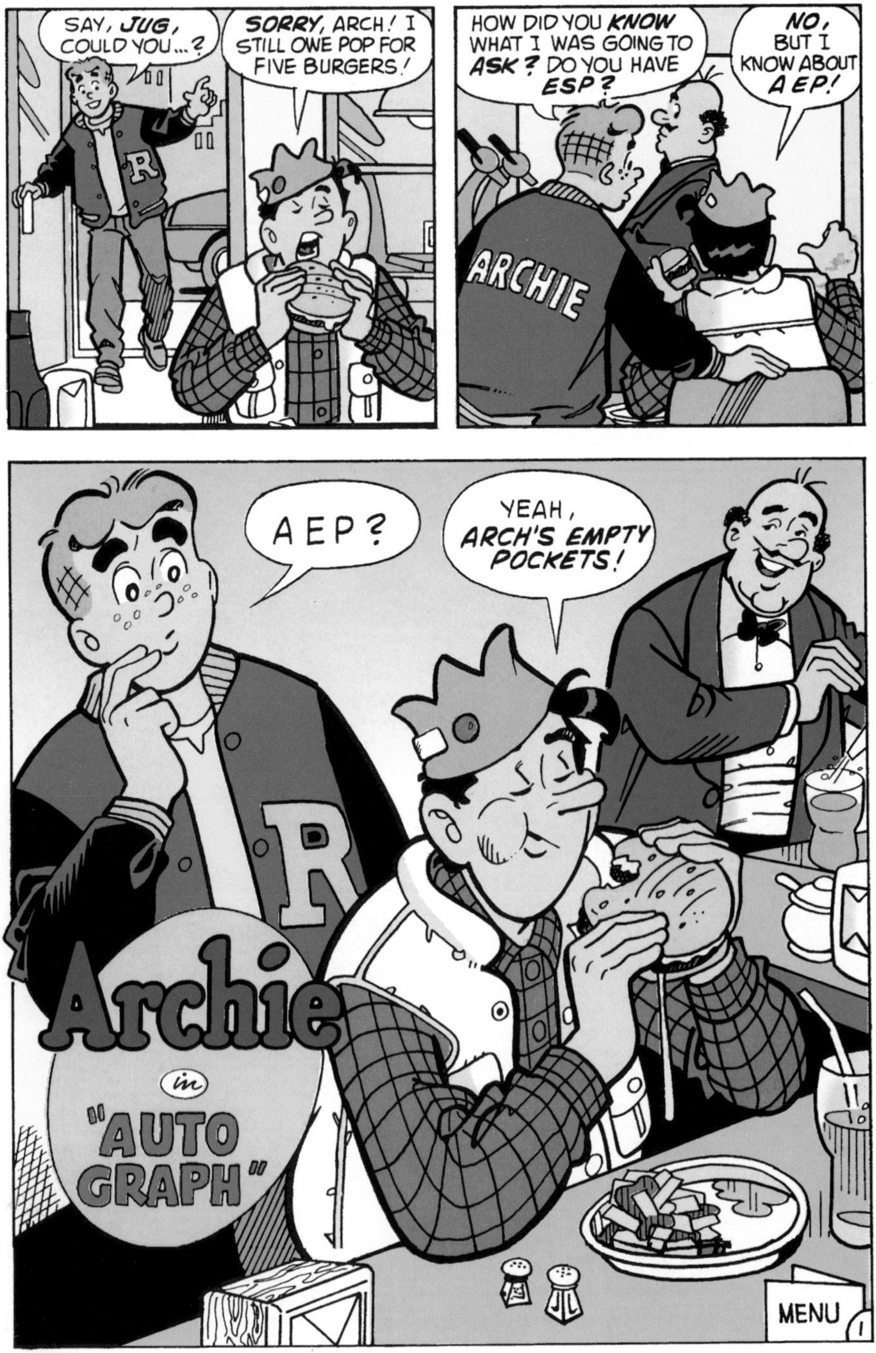
SAY, JUG, COULD YOU...?
SORRY, ARCH! I STILL OWE POP FOR FIVE BURGERS!
HOW DID YOU KNOW WHAT I WAS GOING TO ASK? DO YOU HAVE ESP?
NO, BUT I KNOW ABOUT A EP!
A EP?
YEAH, ARCH'S EMPTY POCKETS!
Archie
in
"AUTO GRAPH"
MENU
1

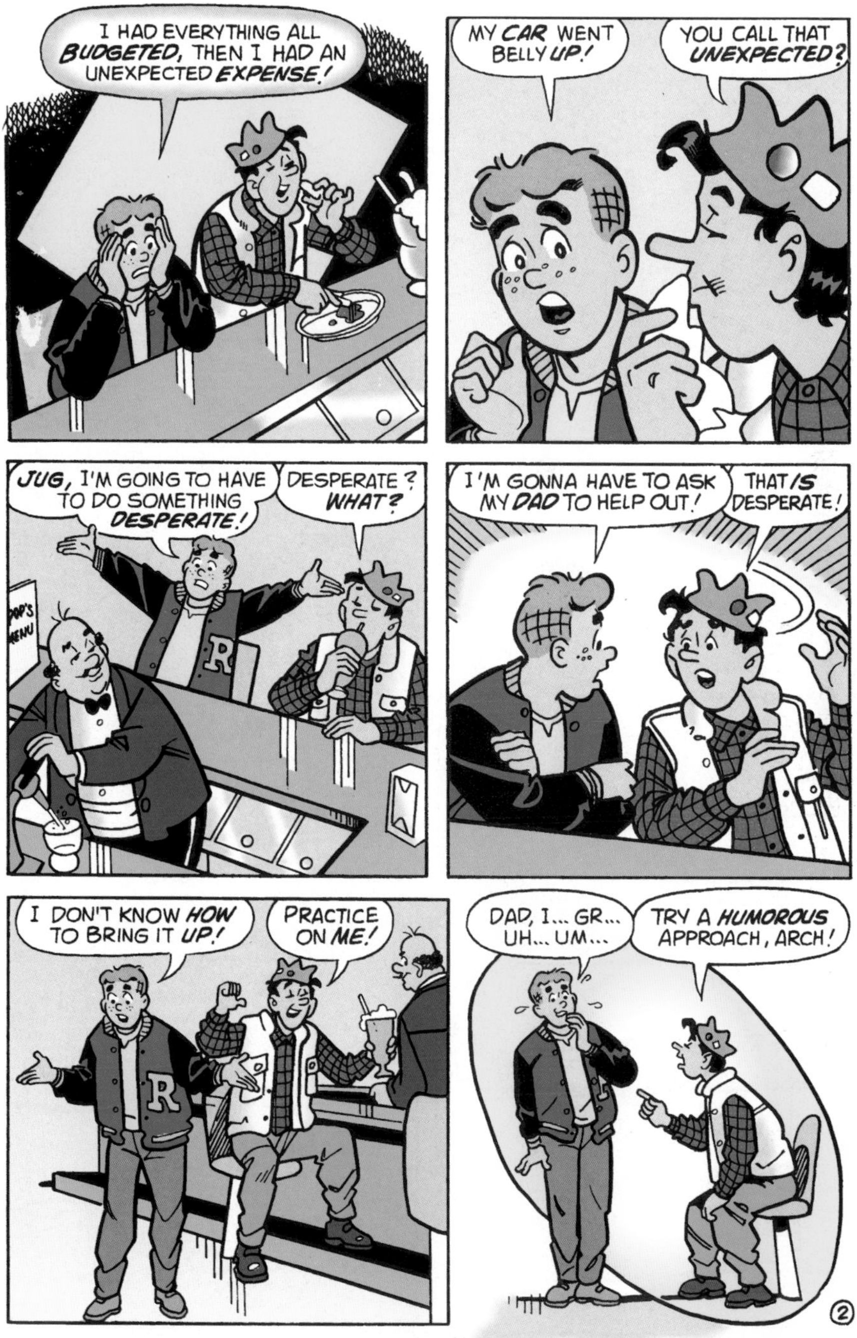
I HAD EVERYTHING ALL BUDGETED, THEN I HAD AN UNEXPECTED EXPENSE!
MY CAR WENT BELLY UP!
YOU CALL THAT UNEXPECTED?
JUG, I'M GOING TO HAVE TO DO SOMETHING DESPERATE!
DESPERATE? WHAT?
POP'S MENU
I'M GONNA HAVE TO ASK MY DAD TO HELP OUT!
THAT IS DESPERATE!
I DON'T KNOW HOW TO BRING IT UP!
PRACTICE ON ME!
DAD, I... GR... UH... UM...
TRY A HUMOROUS APPROACH, ARCH!
2

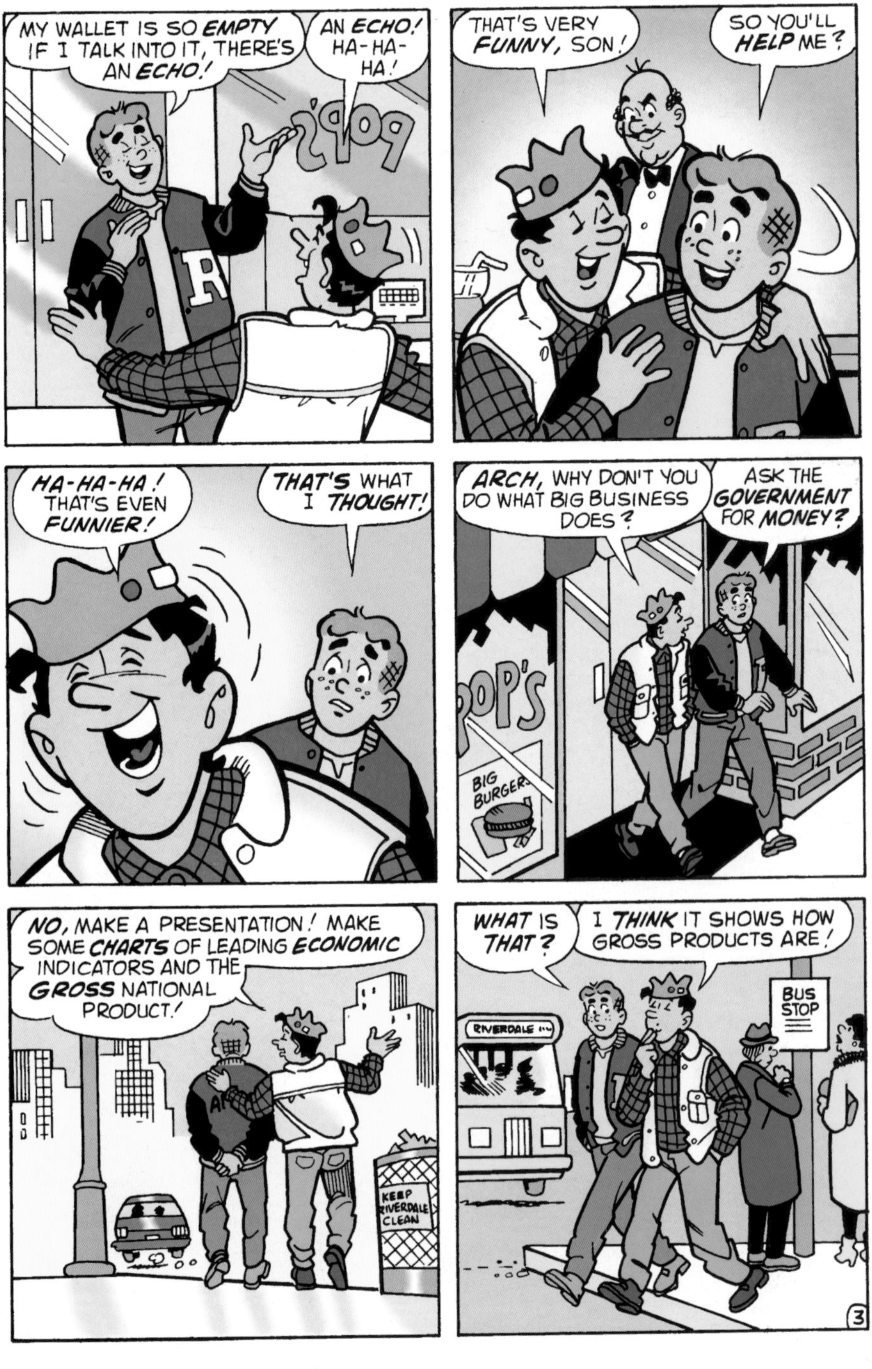
MY WALLET IS SO EMPTY IF I TALK INTO IT, THERE'S AN ECHO!
AN ECHO! HA-HA-HA!
POP'S
THAT'S VERY FUNNY, SON!
SO YOU'LL HELP ME?
HA-HA-HA! THAT'S EVEN FUNNIER!
THAT'S WHAT I THOUGHT!
ARCH, WHY DON'T YOU DO WHAT BIG BUSINESS DOES?
ASK THE GOVERNMENT FOR MONEY?
POP'S
BIG BURGER
NO, MAKE A PRESENTATION! MAKE SOME CHARTS OF LEADING ECONOMIC INDICATORS AND THE GROSS NATIONAL PRODUCT!
KEEP RIVERDALE CLEAN
WHAT IS THAT?
I THINK IT SHOWS HOW GROSS PRODUCTS ARE!
RIVERDALE
BUS STOP
3

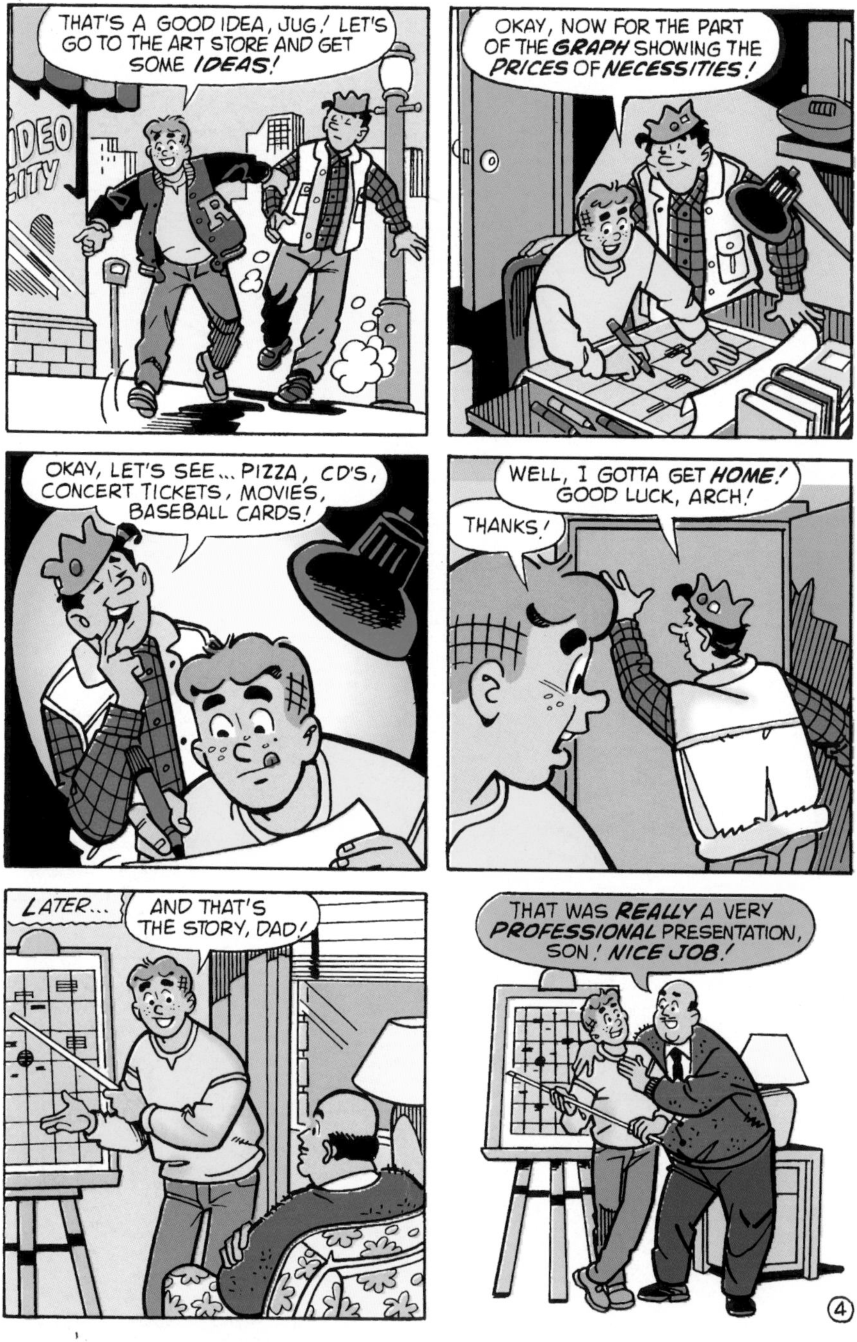
THAT'S A GOOD IDEA, JUG! LET'S GO TO THE ART STORE AND GET SOME *IDEAS*!
IDEO CITY
OKAY, NOW FOR THE PART OF THE *GRAPH* SHOWING THE *PRICES* OF *NECESSITIES*!
OKAY, LET'S SEE... PIZZA, CD'S, CONCERT TICKETS, MOVIES, BASEBALL CARDS!
WELL, I GOTTA GET *HOME*! GOOD LUCK, ARCH!
THANKS!
LATER...
AND THAT'S THE STORY, DAD!
THAT WAS *REALLY* A VERY *PROFESSIONAL* PRESENTATION, SON! *NICE JOB*!
4

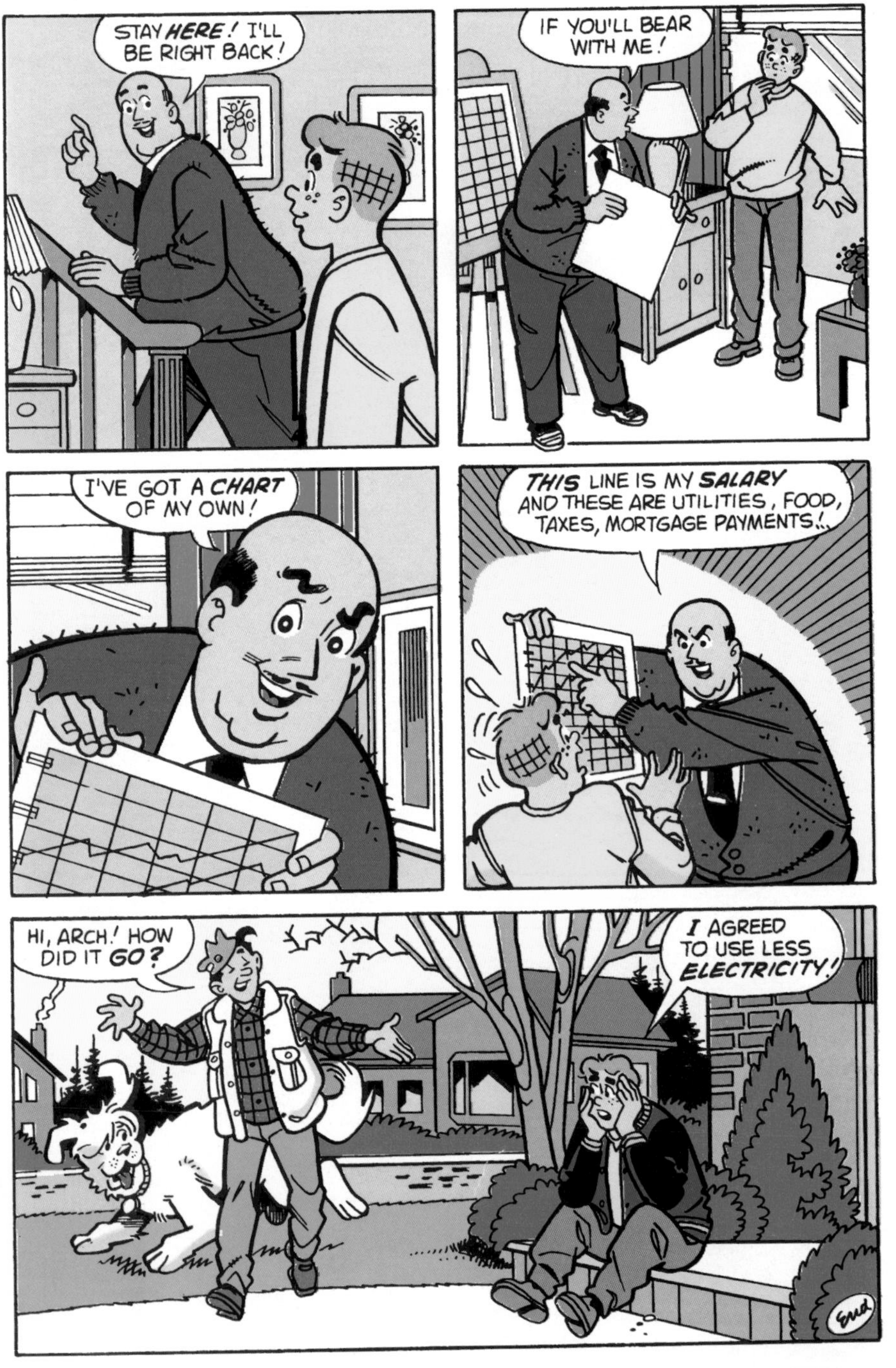
STAY HERE! I'LL BE RIGHT BACK!
IF YOU'LL BEAR WITH ME!
I'VE GOT A CHART OF MY OWN!
THIS LINE IS MY SALARY AND THESE ARE UTILITIES, FOOD, TAXES, MORTGAGE PAYMENTS!
HI, ARCH! HOW DID IT GO?
I AGREED TO USE LESS ELECTRICITY!
End

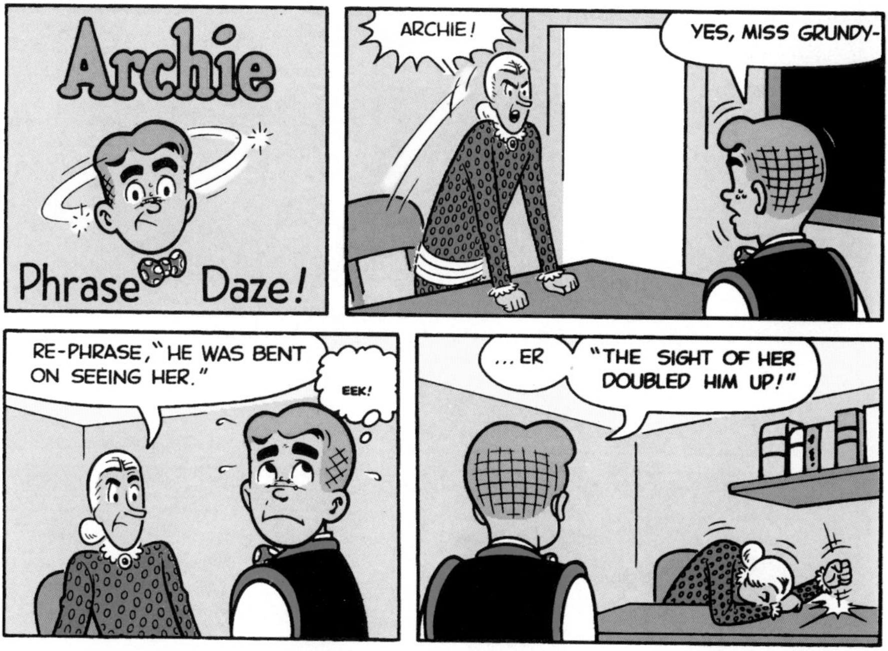
Archie
Phrase Daze!
ARCHIE!
YES, MISS GRUNDY-
RE-PHRASE, "HE WAS BENT ON SEEING HER."
EEK!
...ER
"THE SIGHT OF HER DOUBLED HIM UP!"

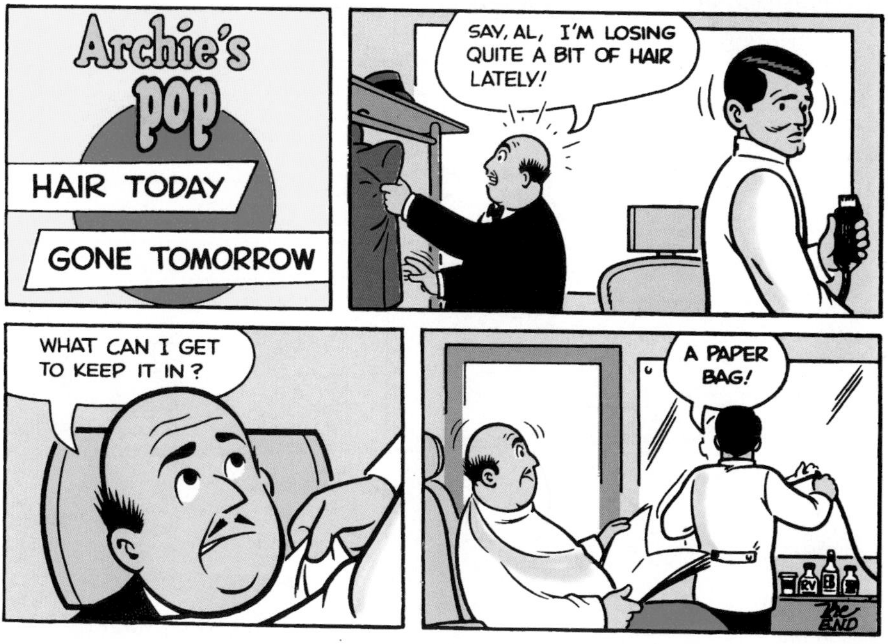
Archie's pop
HAIR TODAY
GONE TOMORROW
SAY, AL, I'M LOSING QUITE A BIT OF HAIR LATELY!
WHAT CAN I GET TO KEEP IT IN?
A PAPER BAG!
THE END

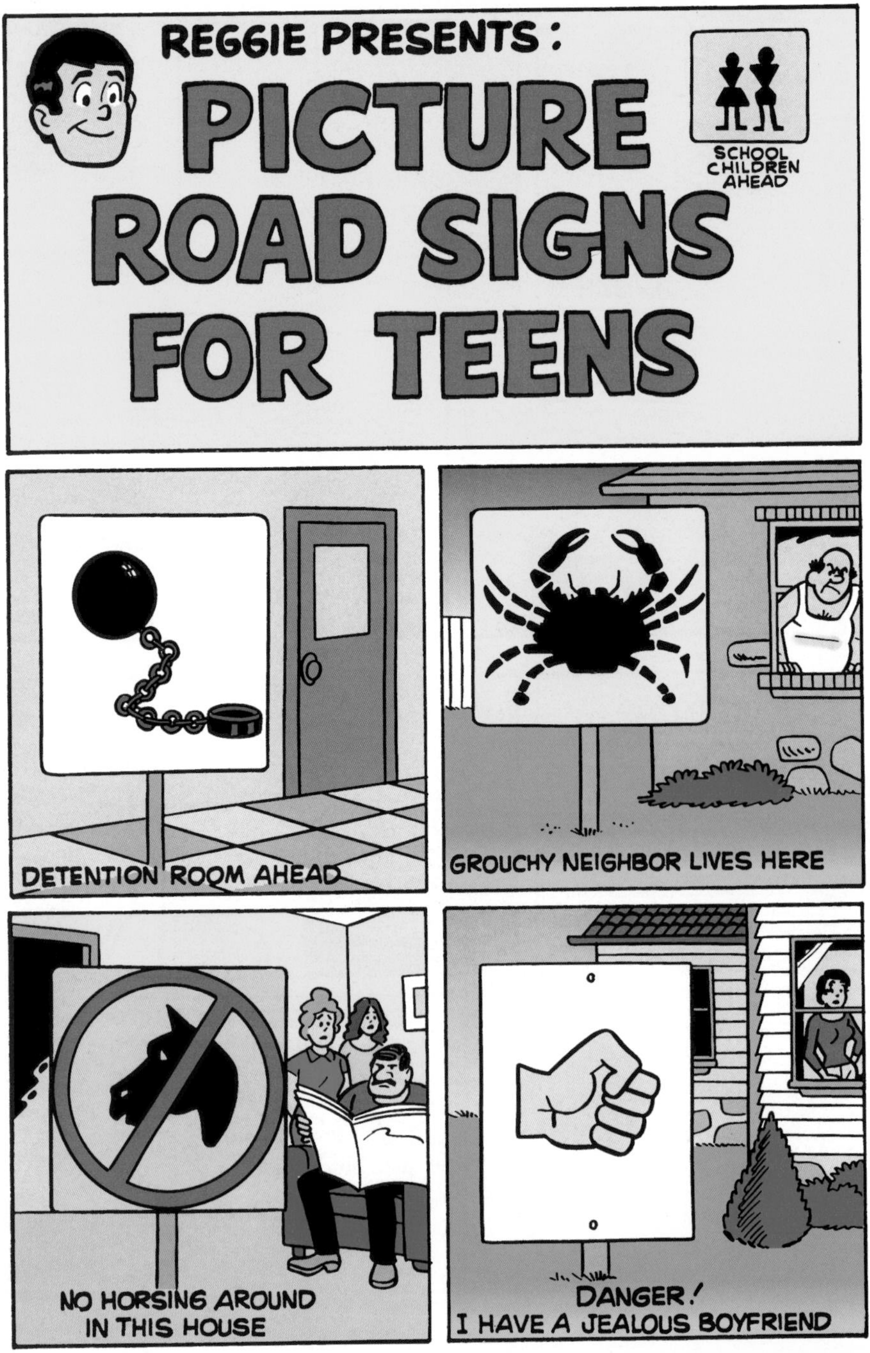
REGGIE PRESENTS:
PICTURE ROAD SIGNS FOR TEENS
SCHOOL CHILDREN AHEAD
DETENTION ROOM AHEAD
GROUCHY NEIGHBOR LIVES HERE
NO HORSING AROUND IN THIS HOUSE
DANGER! I HAVE A JEALOUS BOYFRIEND

OCCUPANT ON A DIET

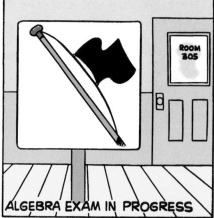

ALGEBRA EXAM IN PROGRESS

BRAGGART LIVES HERE

OCCUPANT WOULD LIKE TO BORROW MONEY

JUST RECEIVED MY ALLOWANCE

JUST SPENT MY ALLOWANCE

END

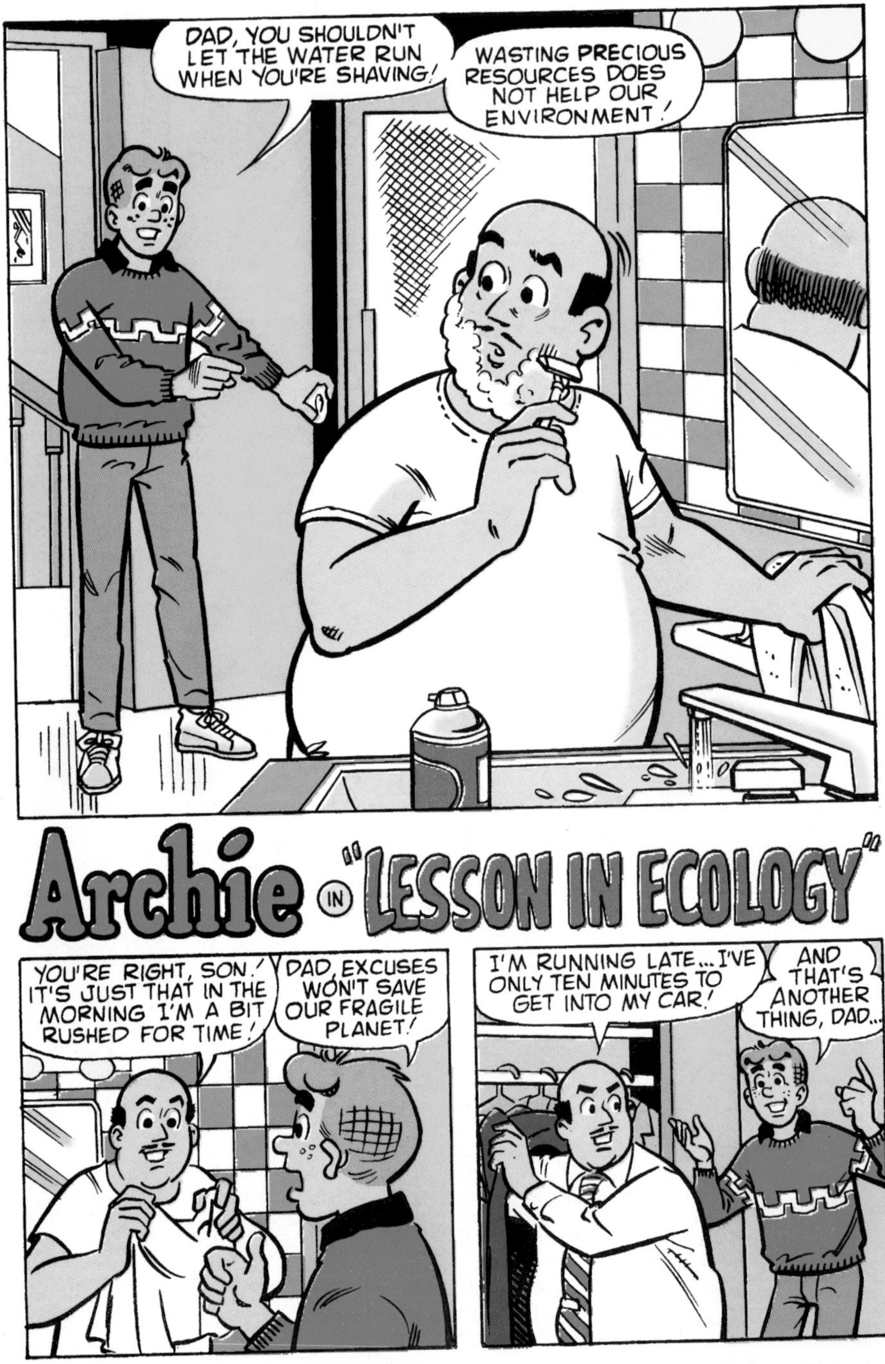
DAD, YOU SHOULDN'T LET THE WATER RUN WHEN YOU'RE SHAVING!
WASTING PRECIOUS RESOURCES DOES NOT HELP OUR ENVIRONMENT!
Archie IN "LESSON IN ECOLOGY"
YOU'RE RIGHT, SON! IT'S JUST THAT IN THE MORNING I'M A BIT RUSHED FOR TIME!
DAD, EXCUSES WON'T SAVE OUR FRAGILE PLANET!
I'M RUNNING LATE... I'VE ONLY TEN MINUTES TO GET INTO MY CAR!
AND THAT'S ANOTHER THING, DAD...

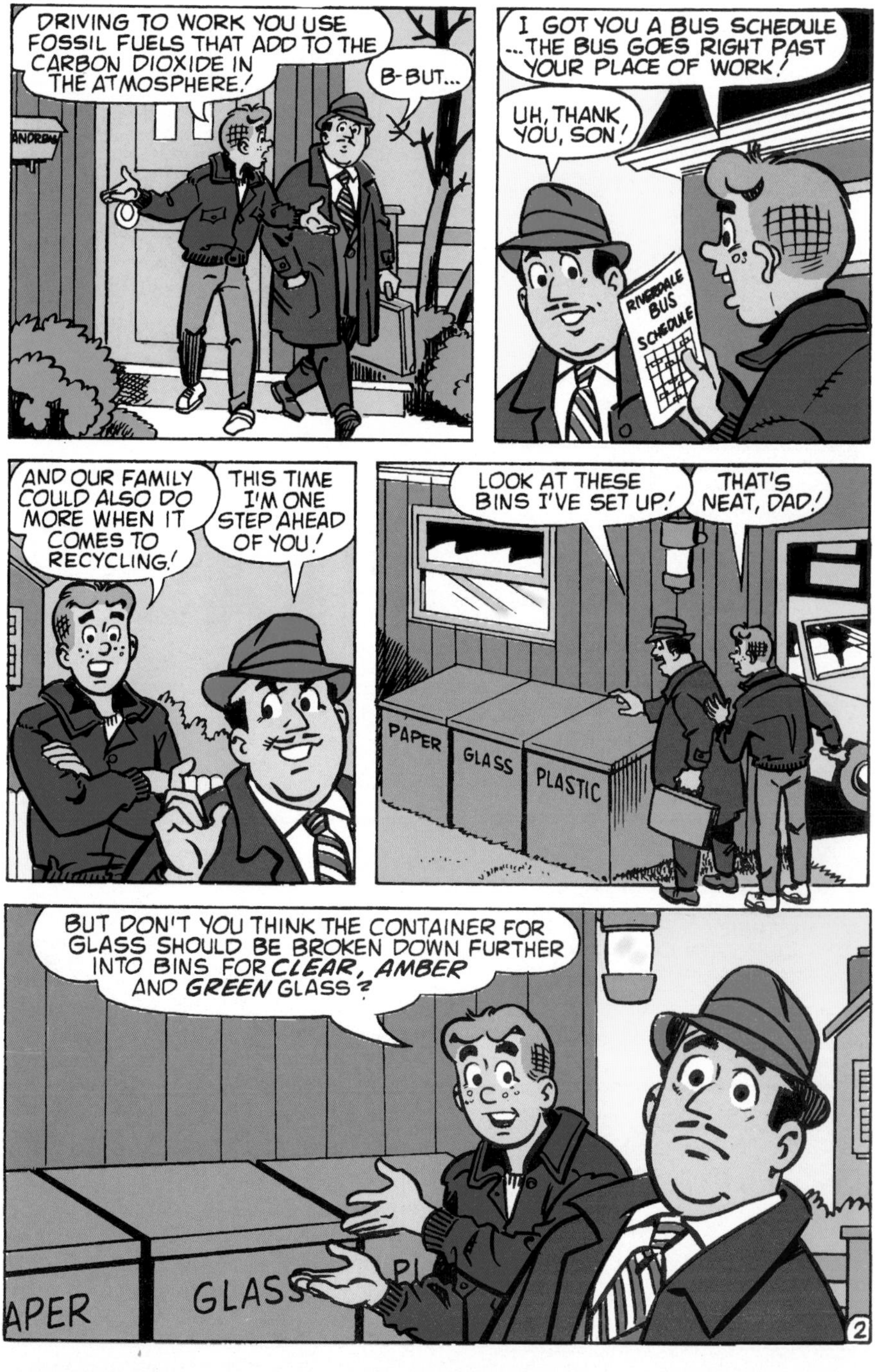
DRIVING TO WORK YOU USE FOSSIL FUELS THAT ADD TO THE CARBON DIOXIDE IN THE ATMOSPHERE!
B-BUT...
ANDREWS
I GOT YOU A BUS SCHEDULE ...THE BUS GOES RIGHT PAST YOUR PLACE OF WORK!
UH, THANK YOU, SON!
RIVERDALE BUS SCHEDULE
AND OUR FAMILY COULD ALSO DO MORE WHEN IT COMES TO RECYCLING!
THIS TIME I'M ONE STEP AHEAD OF YOU!
LOOK AT THESE BINS I'VE SET UP!
THAT'S NEAT, DAD!
PAPER
GLASS
PLASTIC
BUT DON'T YOU THINK THE CONTAINER FOR GLASS SHOULD BE BROKEN DOWN FURTHER INTO BINS FOR *CLEAR, AMBER* AND *GREEN* GLASS?
APER
GLASS
2

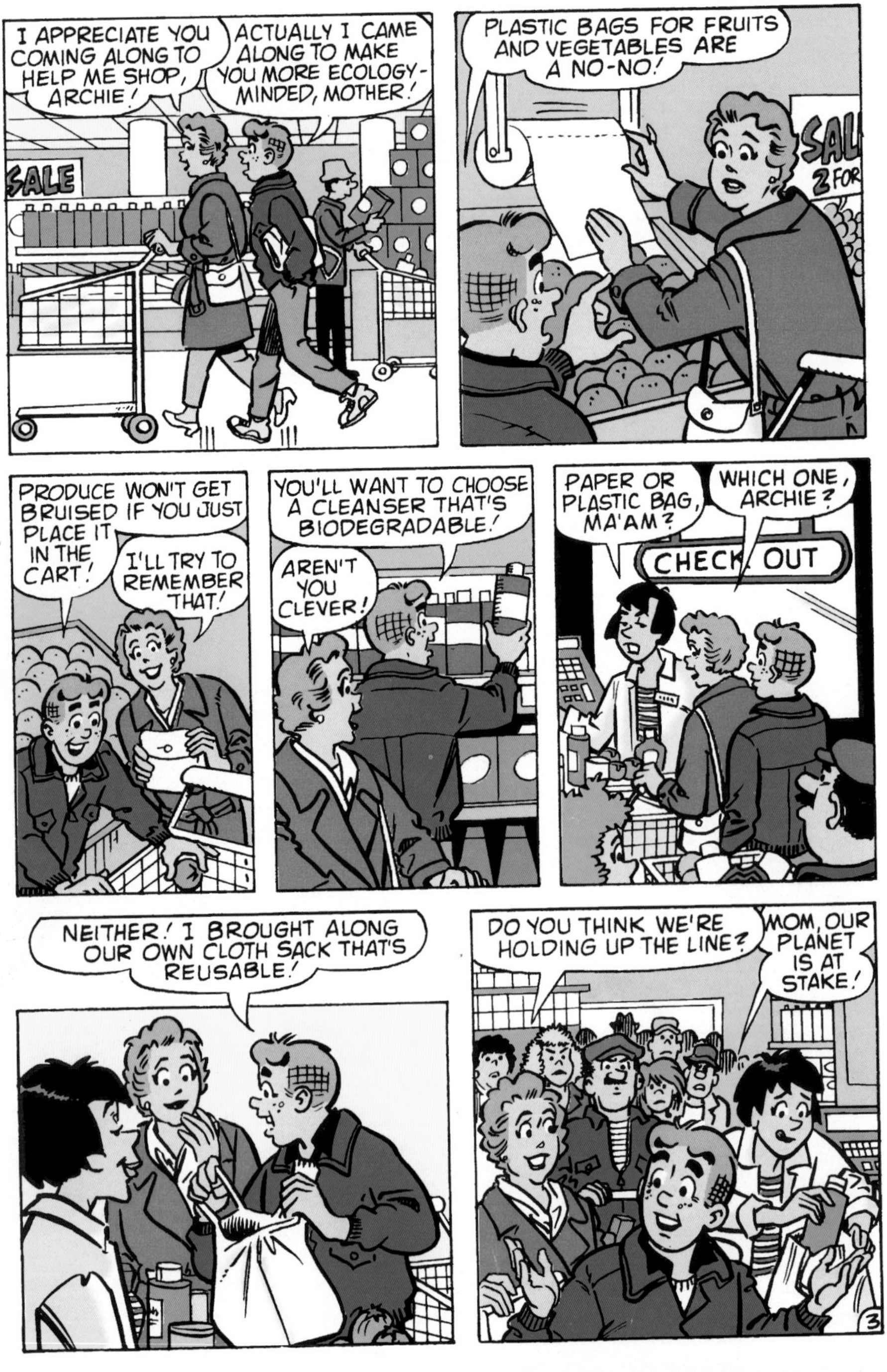
I APPRECIATE YOU COMING ALONG TO HELP ME SHOP, ARCHIE!
ACTUALLY I CAME ALONG TO MAKE YOU MORE ECOLOGY-MINDED, MOTHER!
SALE
PLASTIC BAGS FOR FRUITS AND VEGETABLES ARE A NO-NO!
SALE 2 FOR
PRODUCE WON'T GET BRUISED IF YOU JUST PLACE IT IN THE CART!
I'LL TRY TO REMEMBER THAT!
YOU'LL WANT TO CHOOSE A CLEANSER THAT'S BIODEGRADABLE!
AREN'T YOU CLEVER!
PAPER OR PLASTIC BAG, MA'AM?
WHICH ONE, ARCHIE?
CHECK OUT
NEITHER! I BROUGHT ALONG OUR OWN CLOTH SACK THAT'S REUSABLE!
DO YOU THINK WE'RE HOLDING UP THE LINE?
MOM, OUR PLANET IS AT STAKE!
3

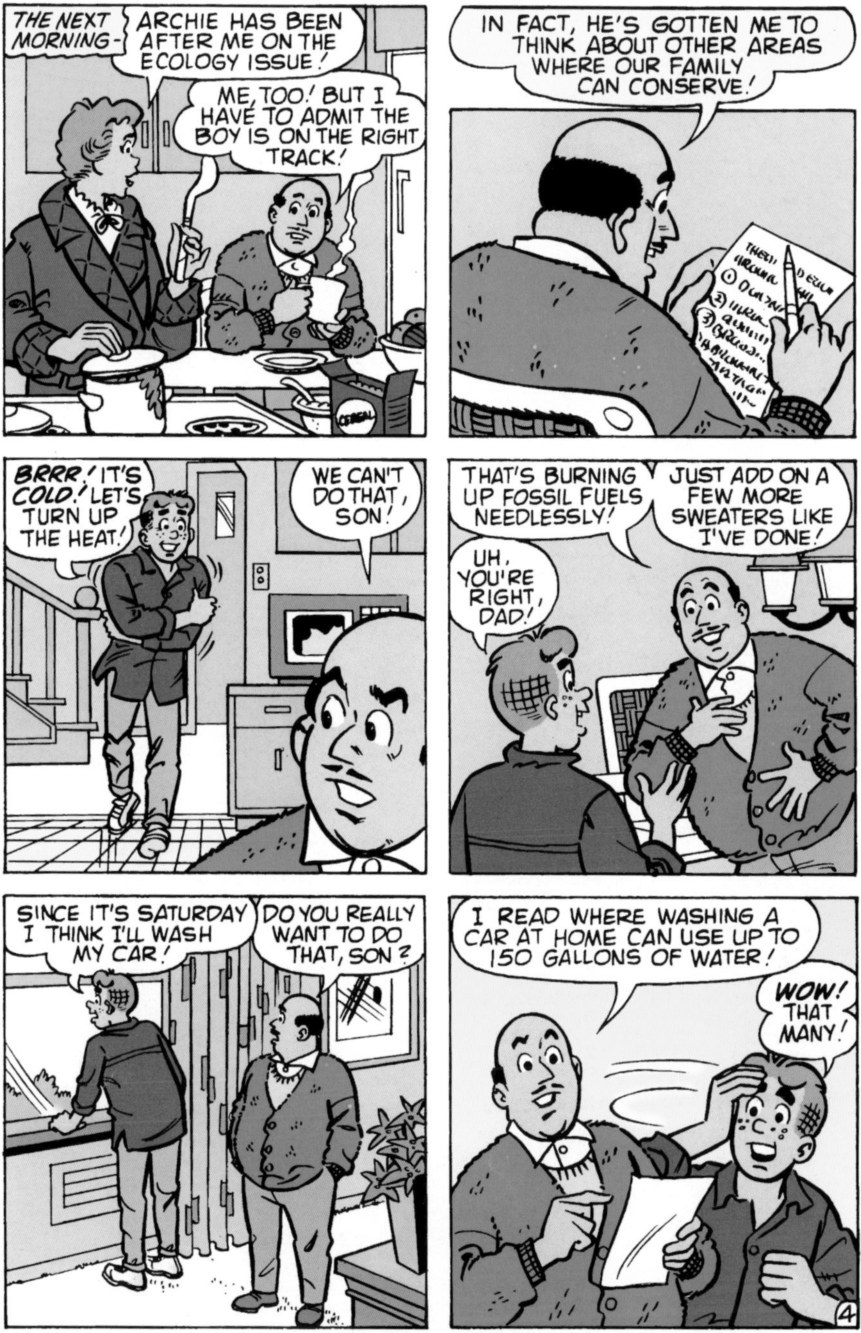
THE NEXT MORNING-
ARCHIE HAS BEEN AFTER ME ON THE ECOLOGY ISSUE!
ME, TOO! BUT I HAVE TO ADMIT THE BOY IS ON THE RIGHT TRACK!
IN FACT, HE'S GOTTEN ME TO THINK ABOUT OTHER AREAS WHERE OUR FAMILY CAN CONSERVE!
CEREAL
BRRR! IT'S COLD! LET'S TURN UP THE HEAT!
WE CAN'T DO THAT, SON!
THAT'S BURNING UP FOSSIL FUELS NEEDLESSLY!
JUST ADD ON A FEW MORE SWEATERS LIKE I'VE DONE!
UH, YOU'RE RIGHT, DAD!
SINCE IT'S SATURDAY I THINK I'LL WASH MY CAR!
DO YOU REALLY WANT TO DO THAT, SON?
I READ WHERE WASHING A CAR AT HOME CAN USE UP TO 150 GALLONS OF WATER!
WOW! THAT MANY!
4

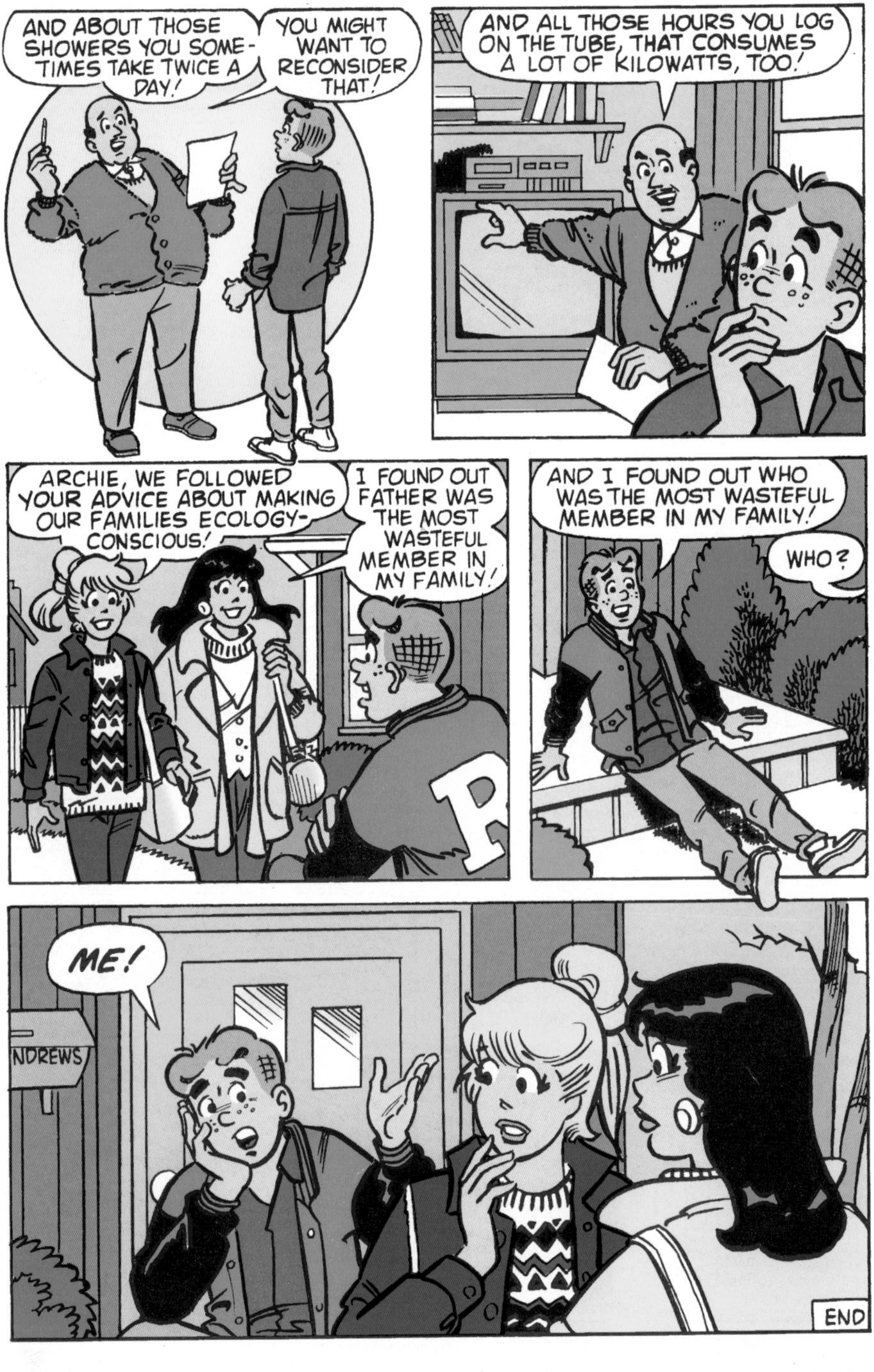
AND ABOUT THOSE SHOWERS YOU SOME-TIMES TAKE TWICE A DAY!
YOU MIGHT WANT TO RECONSIDER THAT!
AND ALL THOSE HOURS YOU LOG ON THE TUBE, THAT CONSUMES A LOT OF KILOWATTS, TOO!
ARCHIE, WE FOLLOWED YOUR ADVICE ABOUT MAKING OUR FAMILIES ECOLOGY-CONSCIOUS!
I FOUND OUT FATHER WAS THE MOST WASTEFUL MEMBER IN MY FAMILY!
AND I FOUND OUT WHO WAS THE MOST WASTEFUL MEMBER IN MY FAMILY!
WHO?
ME!
NDREWS
END

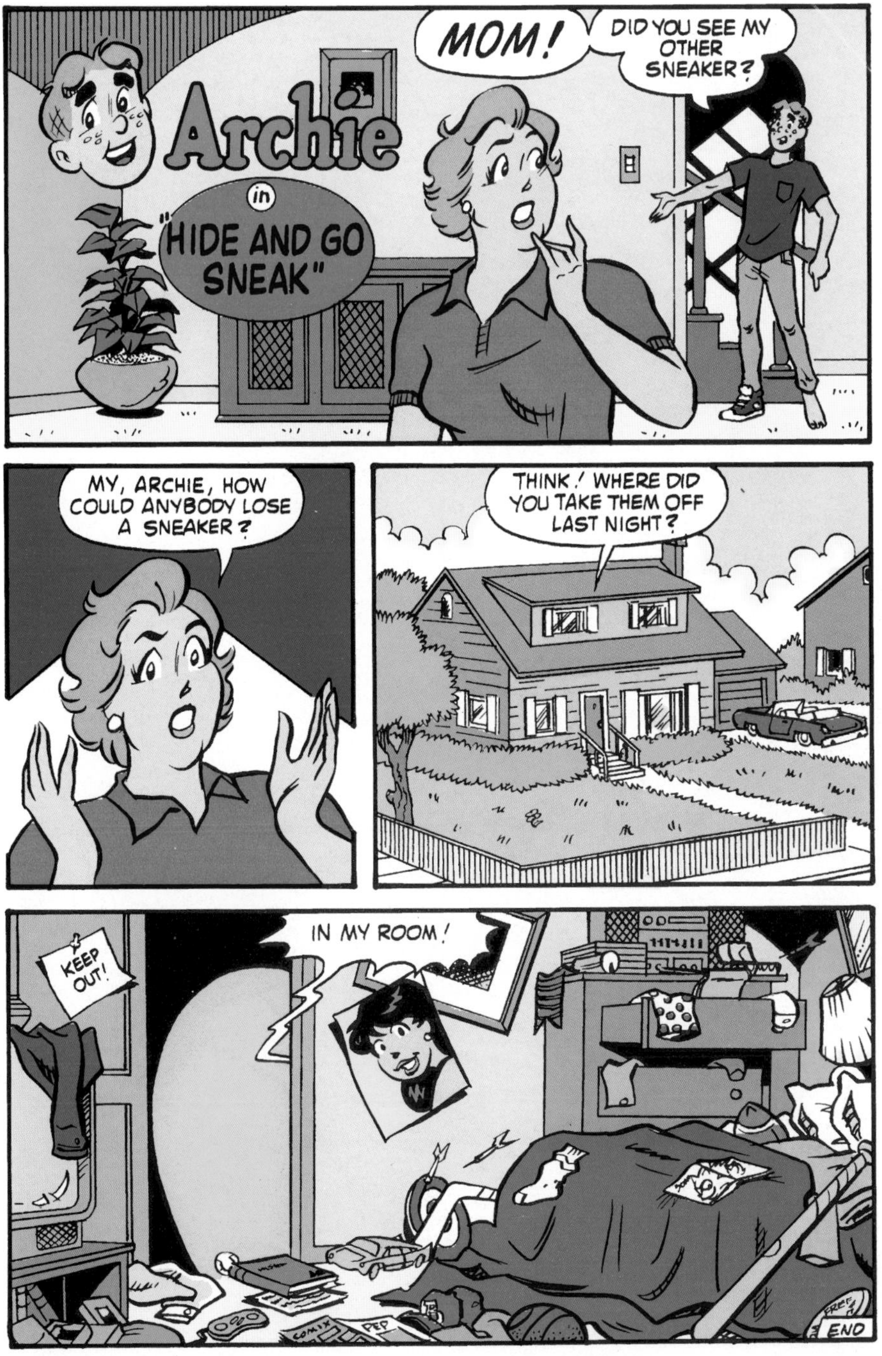
Archie
in
"HIDE AND GO SNEAK"
MOM!
DID YOU SEE MY OTHER SNEAKER?
MY, ARCHIE, HOW COULD ANYBODY LOSE A SNEAKER?
THINK! WHERE DID YOU TAKE THEM OFF LAST NIGHT?
IN MY ROOM!
KEEP OUT!
COMIX
PEP
END

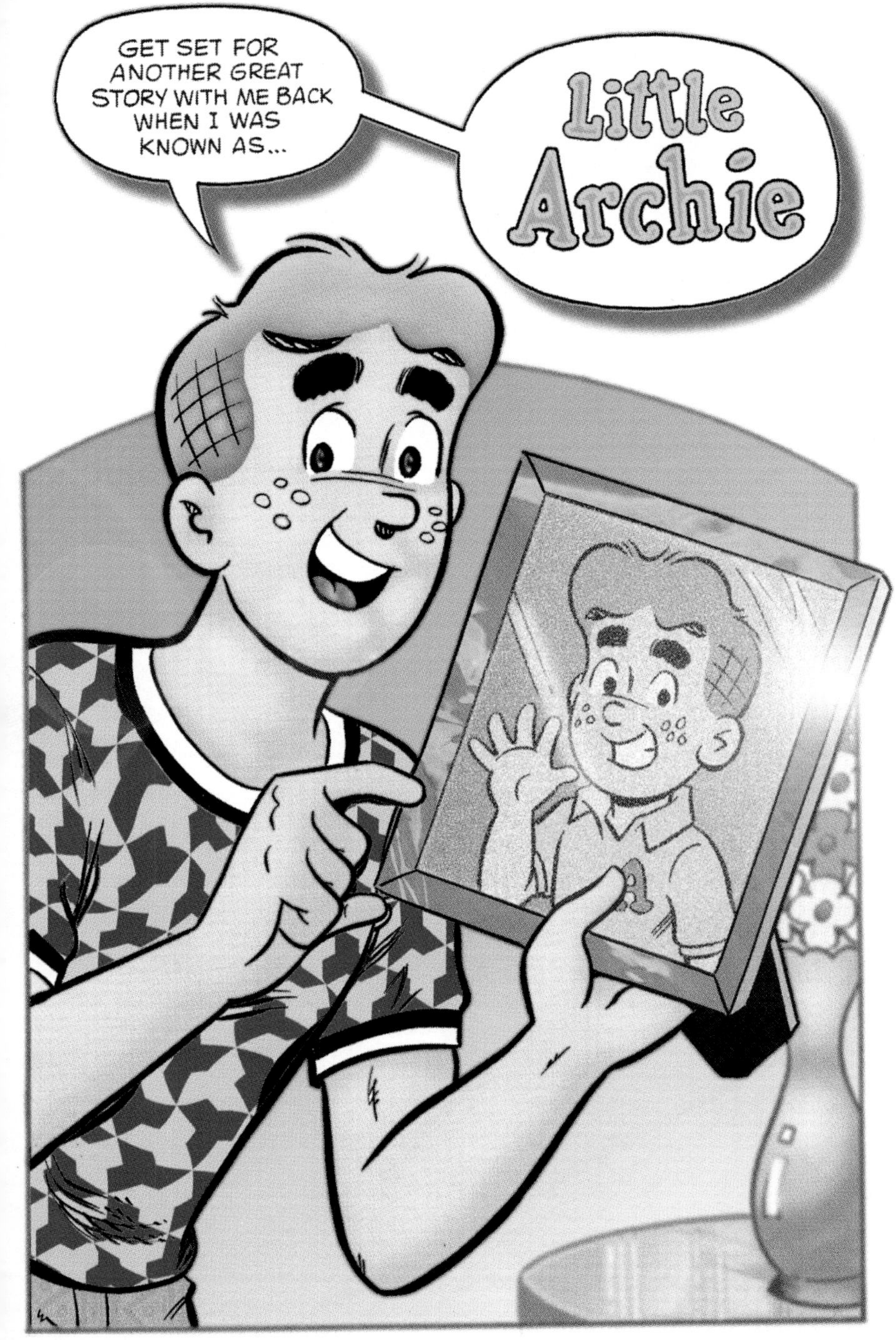
GET SET FOR ANOTHER GREAT STORY WITH ME BACK WHEN I WAS KNOWN AS...
Little Archie

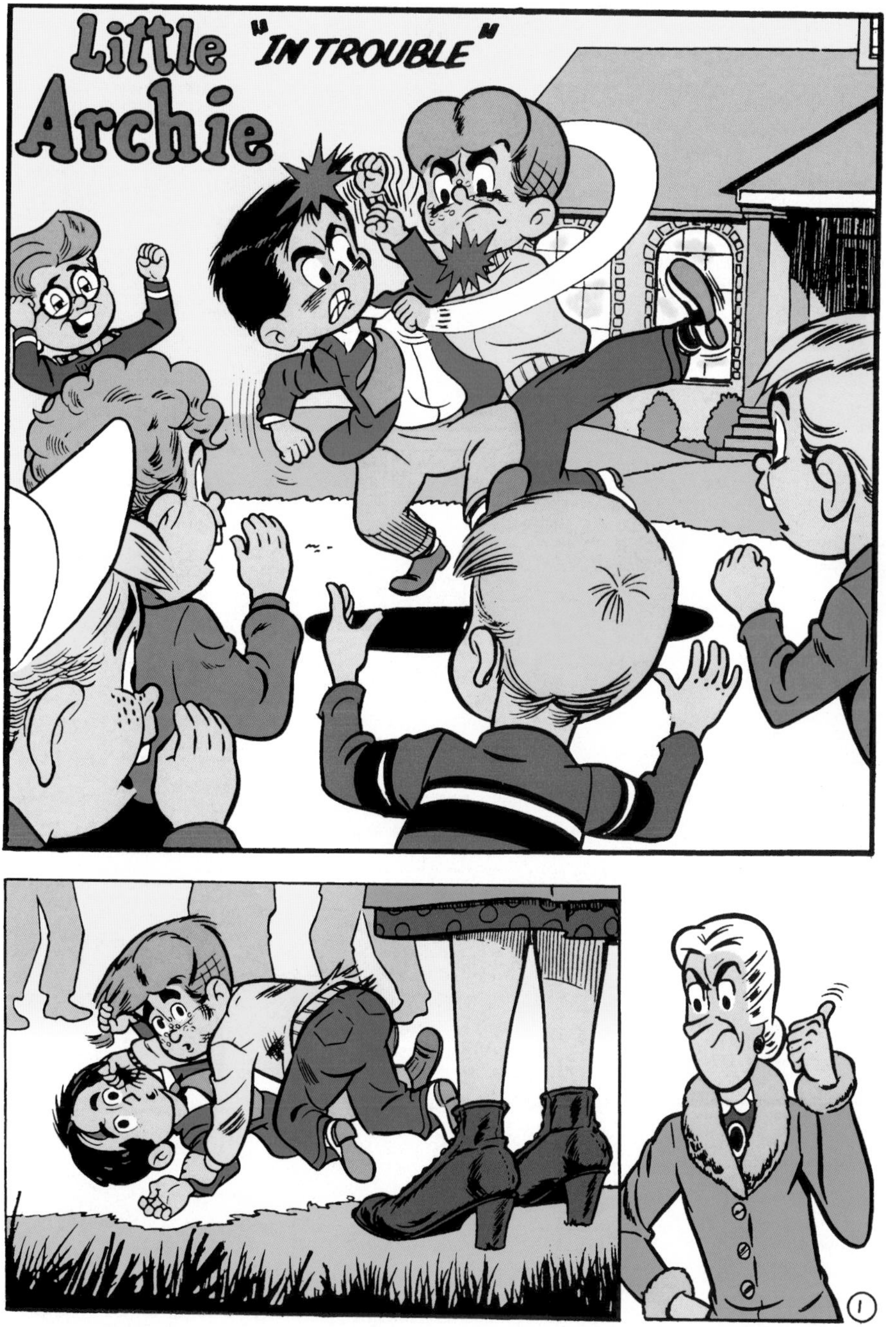
Little Archie
"IN TROUBLE"
1

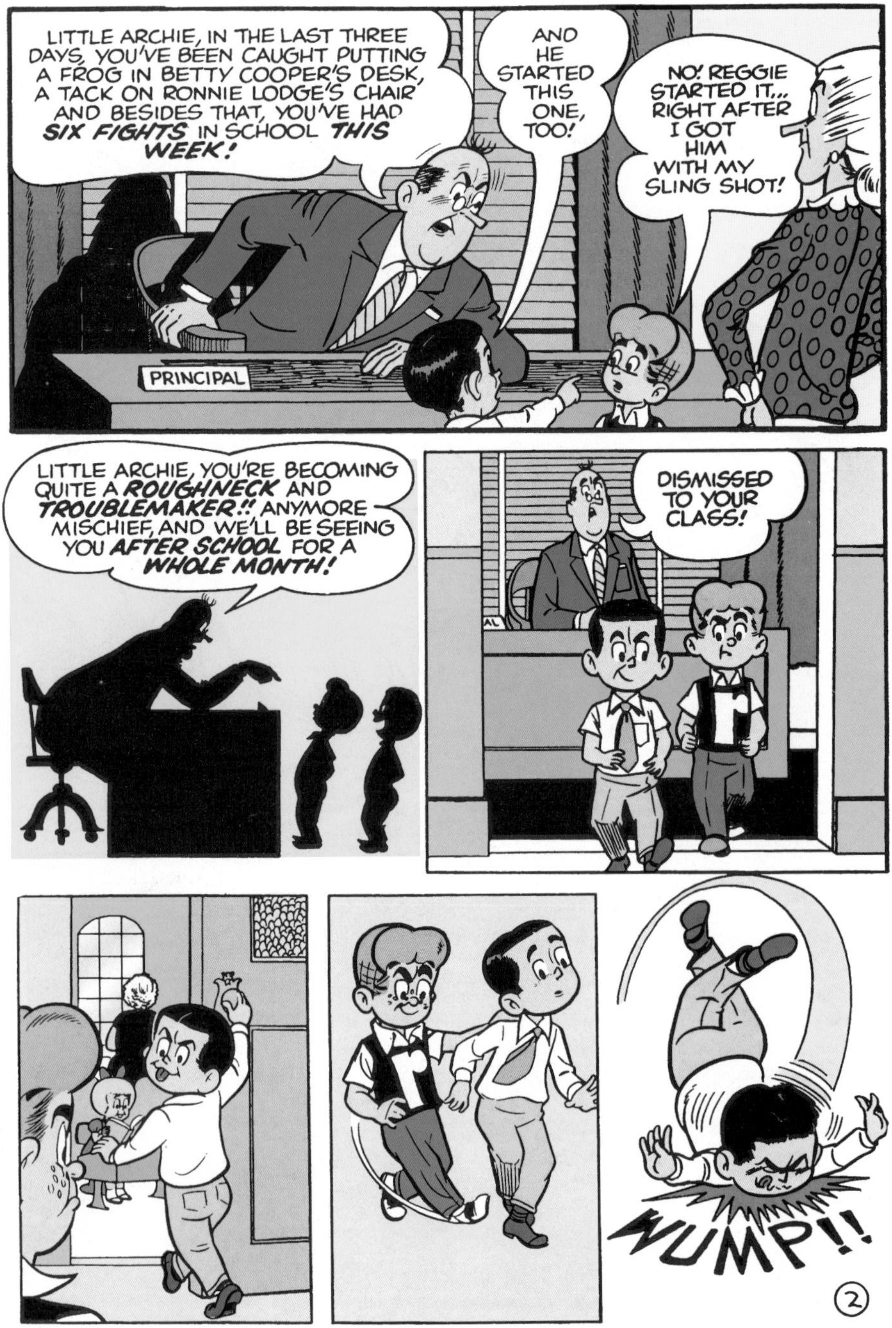
LITTLE ARCHIE, IN THE LAST THREE DAYS, YOU'VE BEEN CAUGHT PUTTING A FROG IN BETTY COOPER'S DESK, A TACK ON RONNIE LODGE'S CHAIR AND BESIDES THAT, YOU'VE HAD SIX FIGHTS IN SCHOOL THIS WEEK!
AND HE STARTED THIS ONE, TOO!
NO! REGGIE STARTED IT... RIGHT AFTER I GOT HIM WITH MY SLING SHOT!
PRINCIPAL
LITTLE ARCHIE, YOU'RE BECOMING QUITE A ROUGHNECK AND TROUBLEMAKER!! ANYMORE MISCHIEF, AND WE'LL BE SEEING YOU AFTER SCHOOL FOR A WHOLE MONTH!
DISMISSED TO YOUR CLASS!
WUMP!!
2

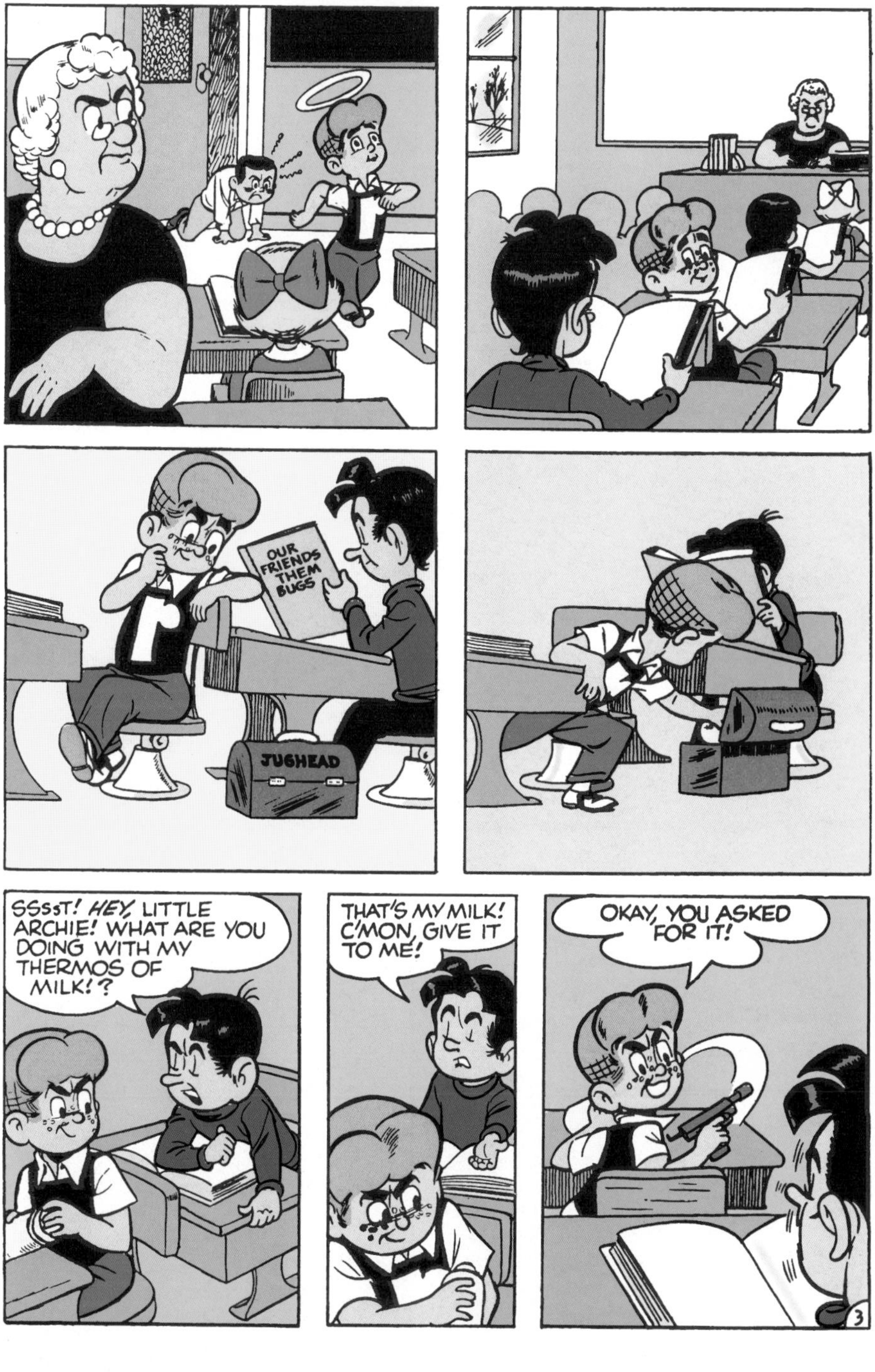
OUR FRIENDS THEM BUGS
JUGHEAD
SSSST! HEY, LITTLE ARCHIE! WHAT ARE YOU DOING WITH MY THERMOS OF MILK!?
THAT'S MY MILK! C'MON, GIVE IT TO ME!
OKAY, YOU ASKED FOR IT!
3

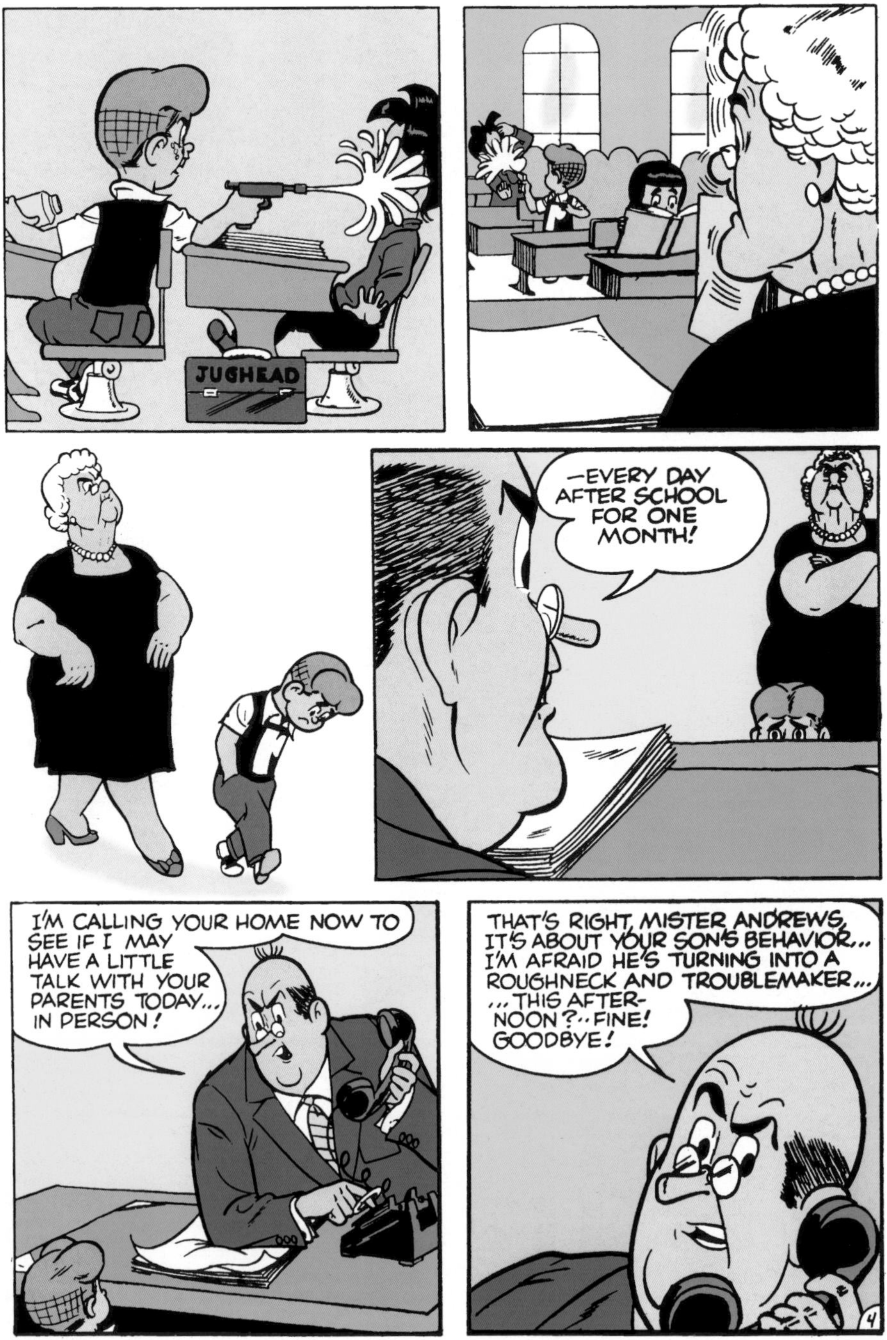
JUGHEAD
—EVERY DAY AFTER SCHOOL FOR ONE MONTH!
I'M CALLING YOUR HOME NOW TO SEE IF I MAY HAVE A LITTLE TALK WITH YOUR PARENTS TODAY... IN PERSON!
THAT'S RIGHT, MISTER ANDREWS, IT'S ABOUT YOUR SON'S BEHAVIOR... I'M AFRAID HE'S TURNING INTO A ROUGHNECK AND TROUBLEMAKER... ...THIS AFTER-NOON?..FINE! GOODBYE!

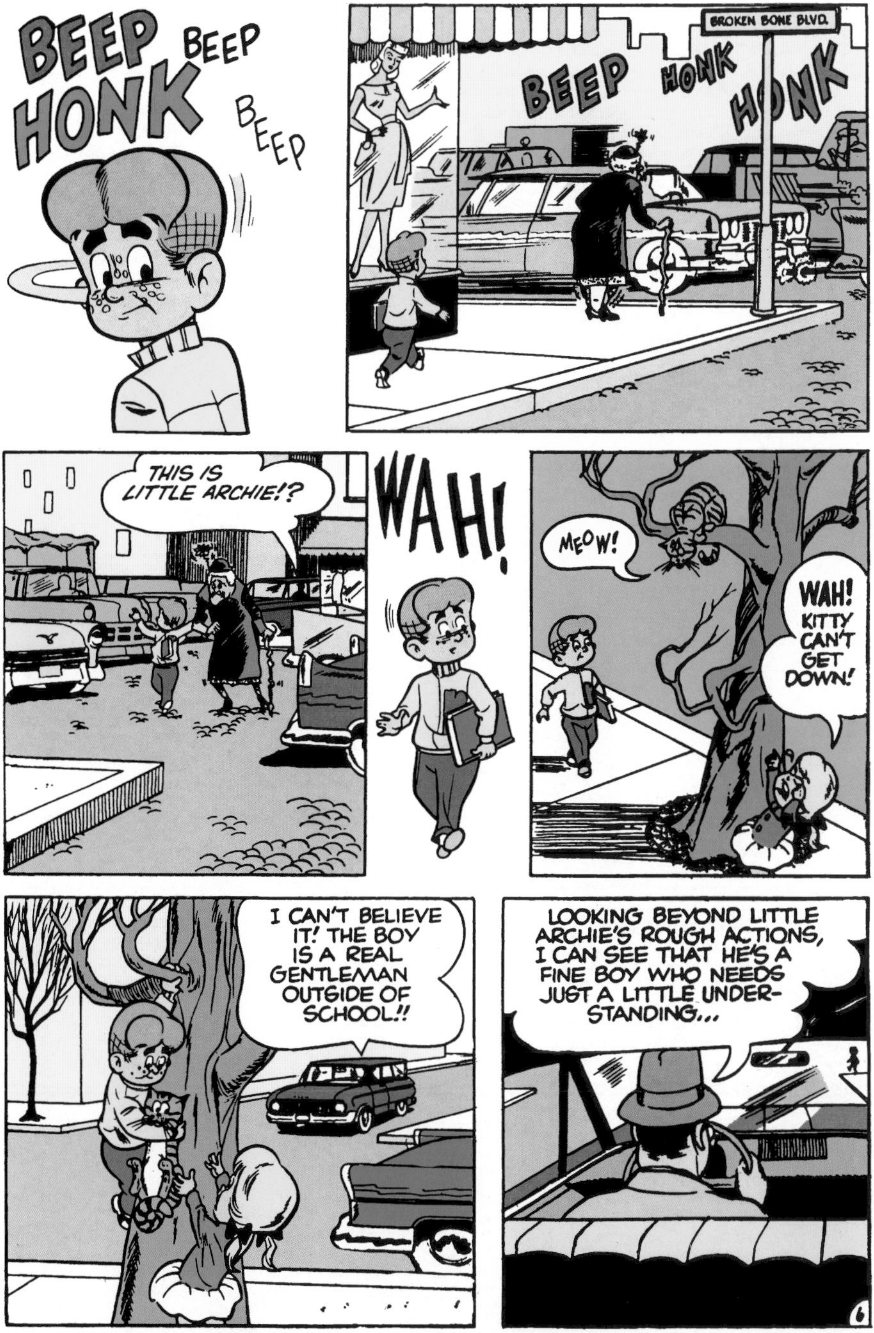
BEEP BEEP
HONK
BEEP
BROKEN BONE BLVD.
BEEP HONK HONK
THIS IS LITTLE ARCHIE!?
WAH!
MEOW!
WAH! KITTY CAN'T GET DOWN!
I CAN'T BELIEVE IT! THE BOY IS A REAL GENTLEMAN OUTSIDE OF SCHOOL!!
LOOKING BEYOND LITTLE ARCHIE'S ROUGH ACTIONS, I CAN SEE THAT HE'S A FINE BOY WHO NEEDS JUST A LITTLE UNDER-STANDING...
6

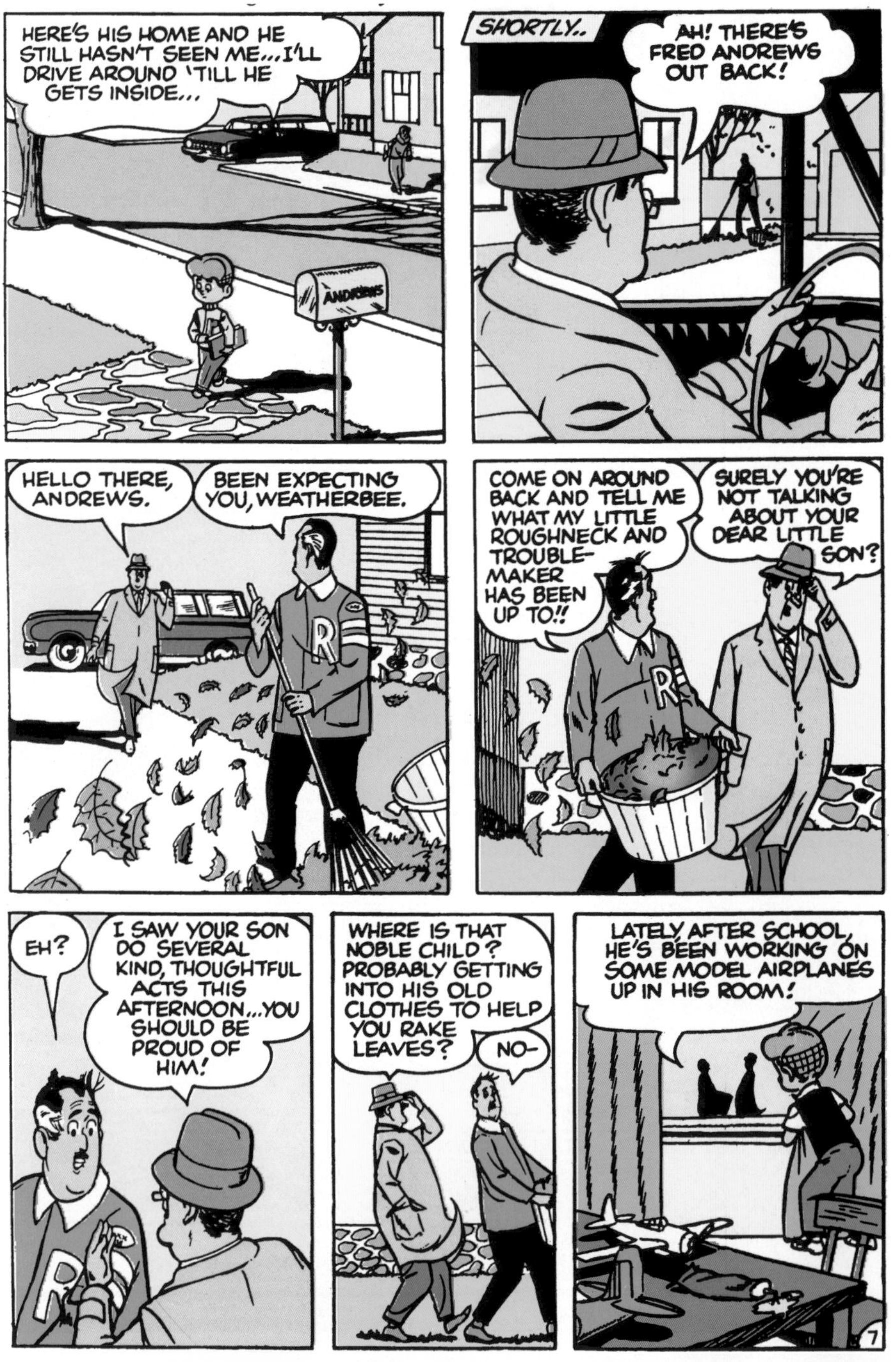
HERE'S HIS HOME AND HE STILL HASN'T SEEN ME...I'LL DRIVE AROUND 'TILL HE GETS INSIDE...
ANDREWS
SHORTLY..
AH! THERE'S FRED ANDREWS OUT BACK!
HELLO THERE, ANDREWS.
BEEN EXPECTING YOU, WEATHERBEE.
COME ON AROUND BACK AND TELL ME WHAT MY LITTLE ROUGHNECK AND TROUBLE-MAKER HAS BEEN UP TO!!
SURELY YOU'RE NOT TALKING ABOUT YOUR DEAR LITTLE SON?
EH?
I SAW YOUR SON DO SEVERAL KIND, THOUGHTFUL ACTS THIS AFTERNOON...YOU SHOULD BE PROUD OF HIM!
WHERE IS THAT NOBLE CHILD? PROBABLY GETTING INTO HIS OLD CLOTHES TO HELP YOU RAKE LEAVES?
NO-
LATELY, AFTER SCHOOL, HE'S BEEN WORKING ON SOME MODEL AIRPLANES UP IN HIS ROOM!
7

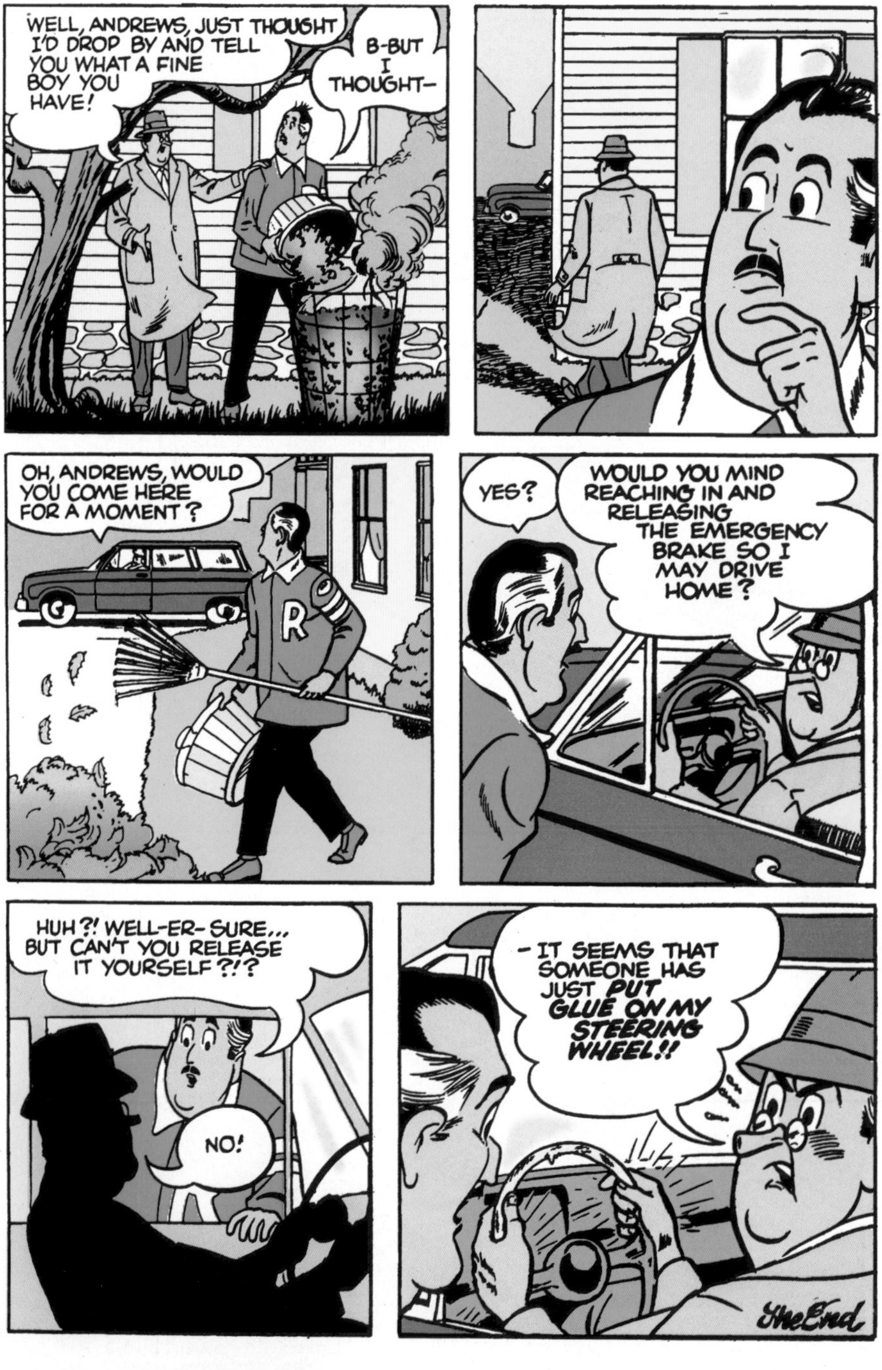
WELL, ANDREWS, JUST THOUGHT I'D DROP BY AND TELL YOU WHAT A FINE BOY YOU HAVE!
B-BUT I THOUGHT-
OH, ANDREWS, WOULD YOU COME HERE FOR A MOMENT?
R
YES?
WOULD YOU MIND REACHING IN AND RELEASING THE EMERGENCY BRAKE SO I MAY DRIVE HOME?
HUH?! WELL-ER-SURE... BUT CAN'T YOU RELEASE IT YOURSELF?!?
NO!
-IT SEEMS THAT SOMEONE HAS JUST PUT GLUE ON MY STEERING WHEEL!!
The End

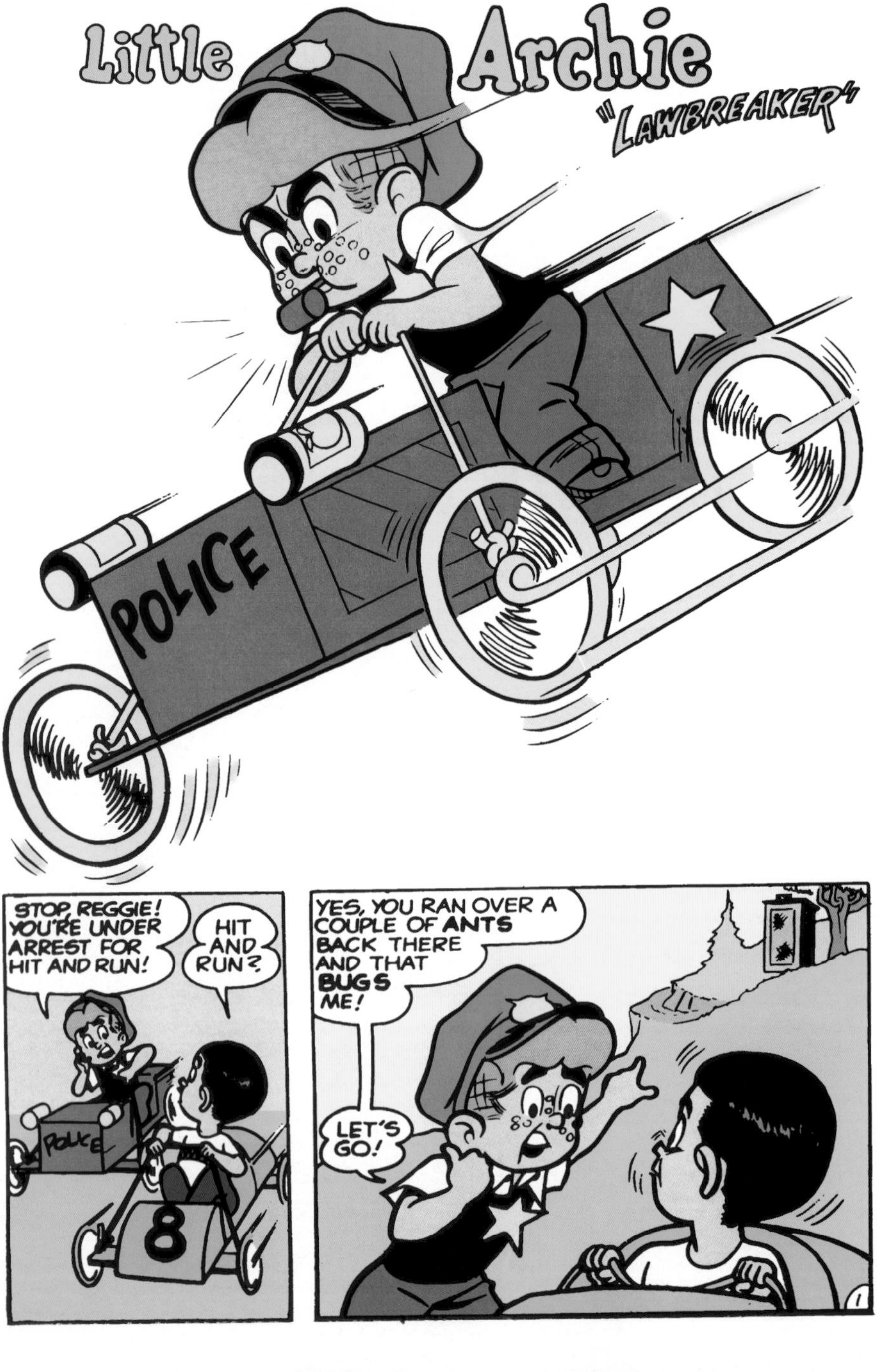
Little Archie
"LAWBREAKER"
POLICE
STOP, REGGIE! YOU'RE UNDER ARREST FOR HIT AND RUN!
HIT AND RUN?
POLICE
8
YES, YOU RAN OVER A COUPLE OF ANTS BACK THERE AND THAT BUGS ME!
LET'S GO!
1

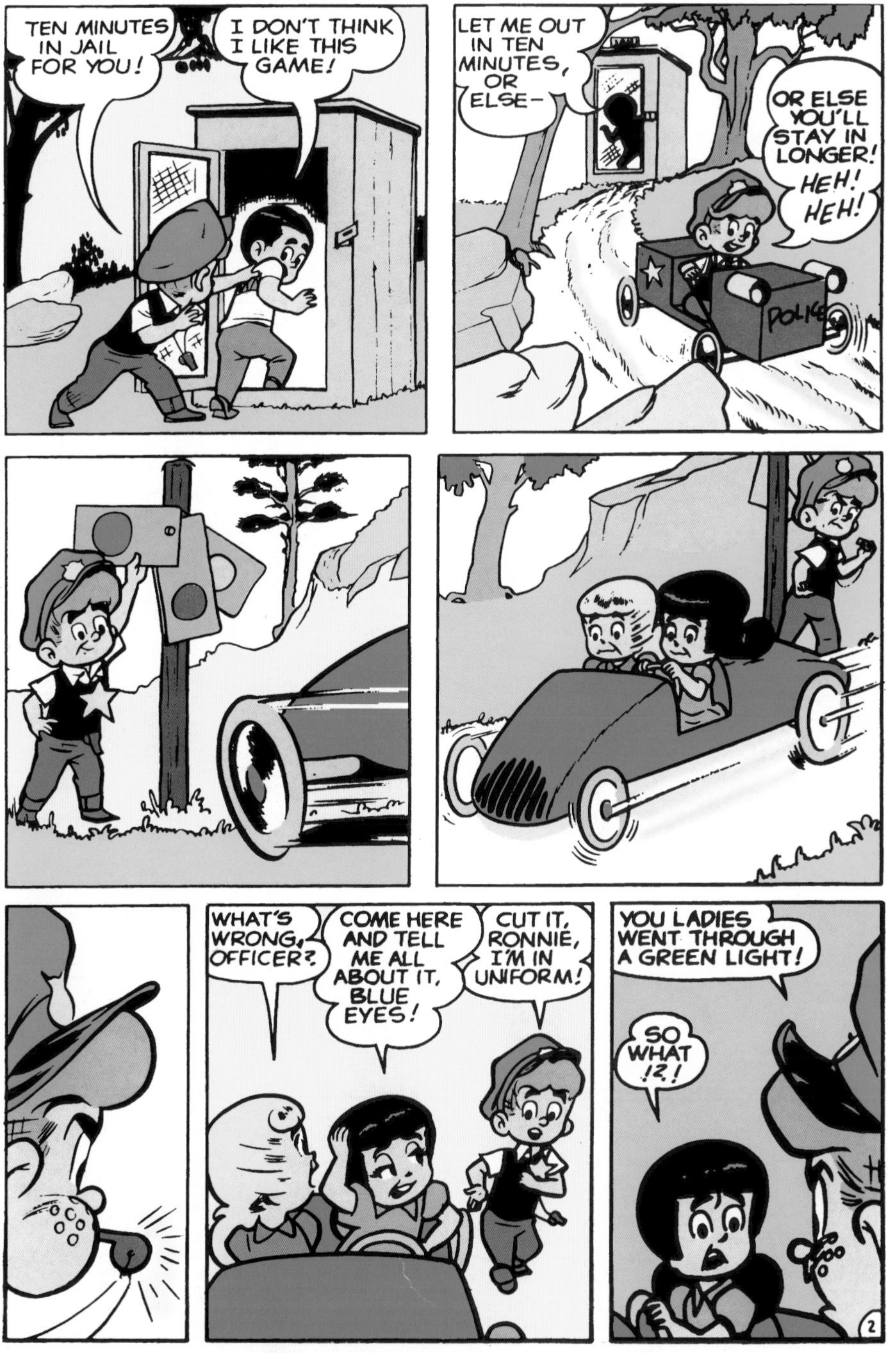
TEN MINUTES IN JAIL FOR YOU!
I DON'T THINK I LIKE THIS GAME!
LET ME OUT IN TEN MINUTES, OR ELSE-
OR ELSE YOU'LL STAY IN LONGER! HEH! HEH!
POLICE
WHAT'S WRONG, OFFICER?
COME HERE AND TELL ME ALL ABOUT IT, BLUE EYES!
CUT IT, RONNIE, I'M IN UNIFORM!
YOU LADIES WENT THROUGH A GREEN LIGHT!
SO WHAT !?!
2

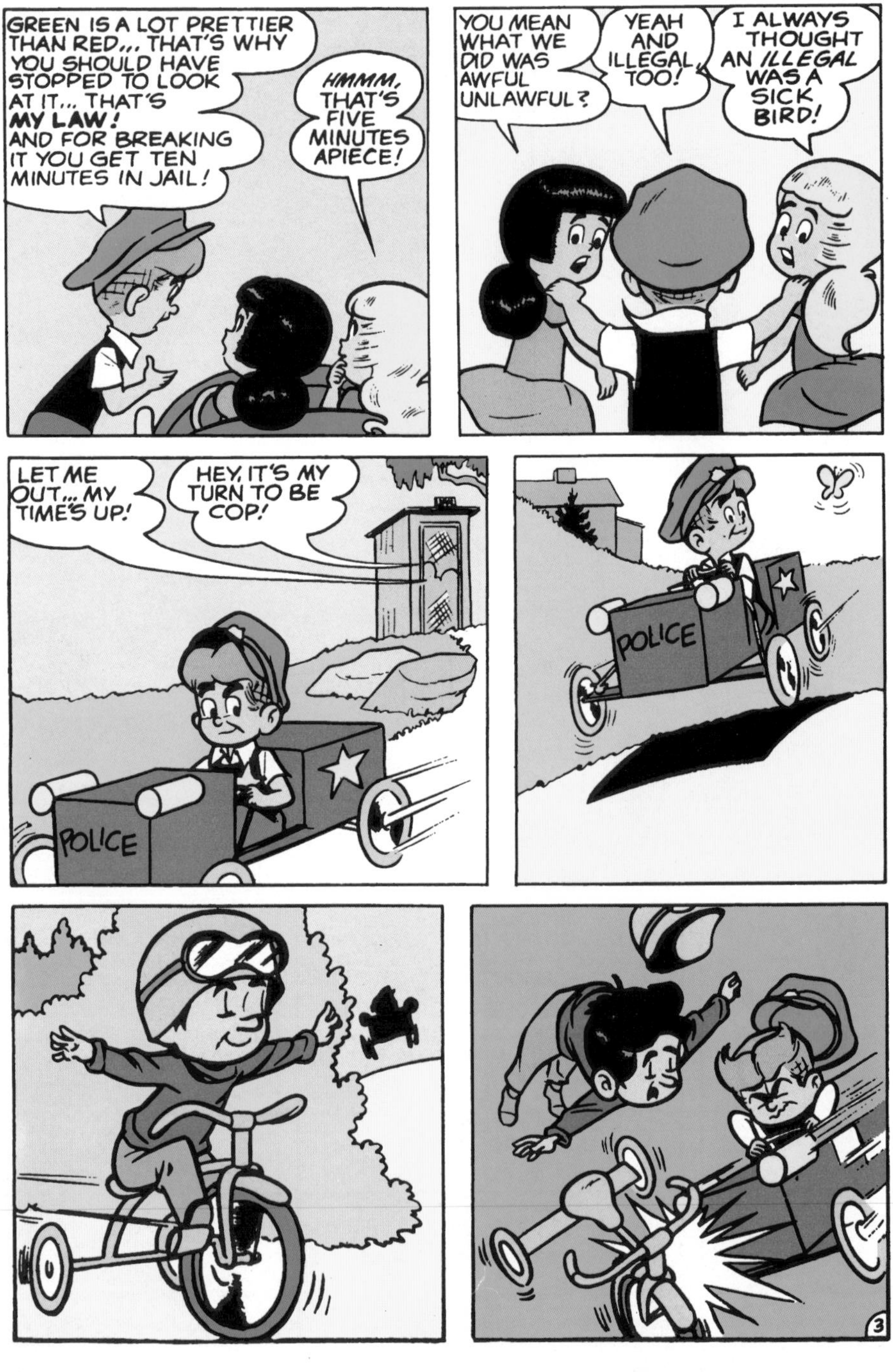
GREEN IS A LOT PRETTIER THAN RED... THAT'S WHY YOU SHOULD HAVE STOPPED TO LOOK AT IT... THAT'S **MY LAW!** AND FOR BREAKING IT YOU GET TEN MINUTES IN JAIL!
HMMM, THAT'S FIVE MINUTES APIECE!
YOU MEAN WHAT WE DID WAS AWFUL UNLAWFUL?
YEAH AND ILLEGAL, TOO!
I ALWAYS THOUGHT AN *ILLEGAL* WAS A SICK BIRD!
LET ME OUT... MY TIME'S UP!
HEY, IT'S MY TURN TO BE COP!
POLICE
POLICE
3

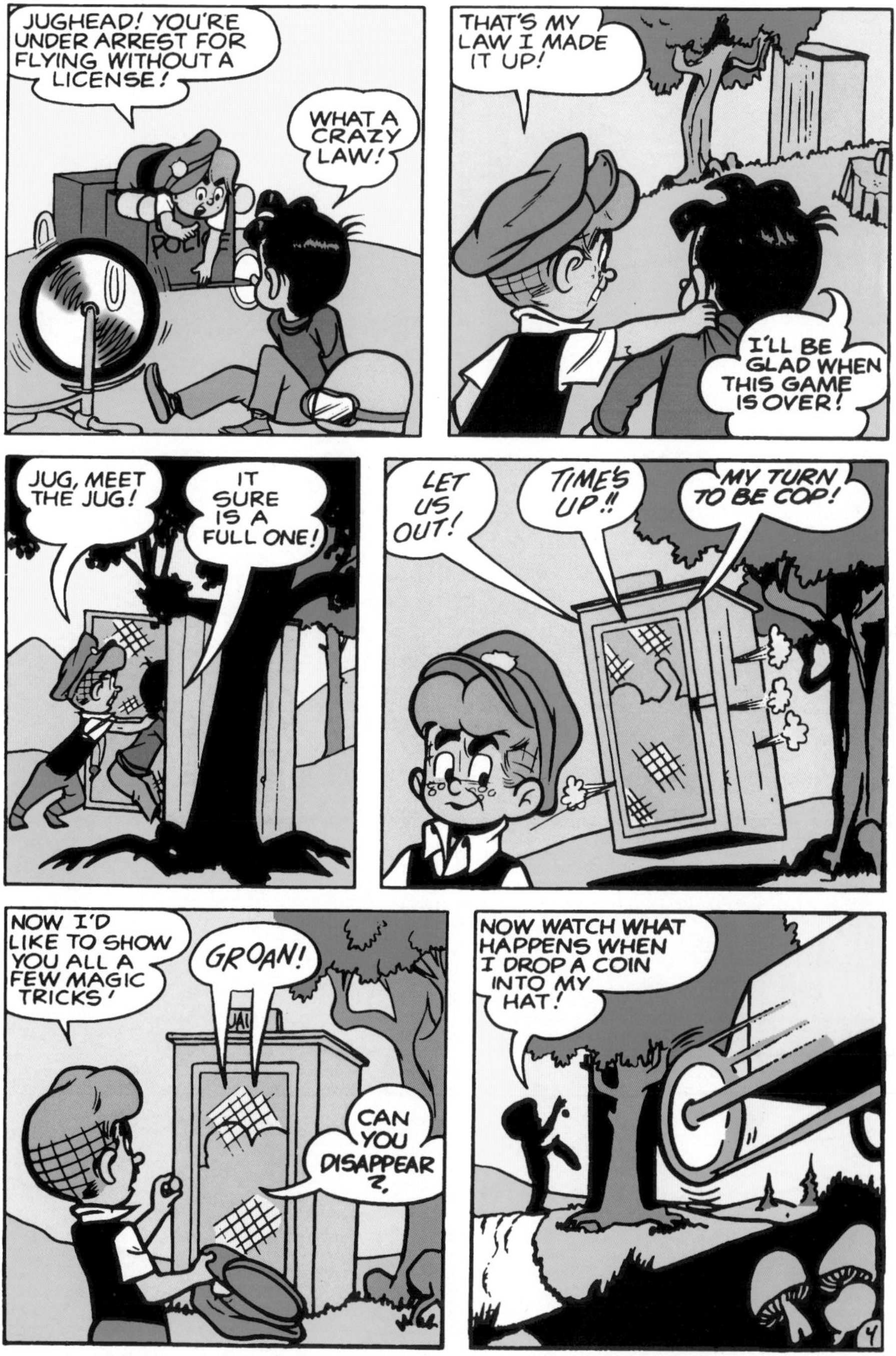
JUGHEAD! YOU'RE UNDER ARREST FOR FLYING WITHOUT A LICENSE!
WHAT A CRAZY LAW!
POLICE
THAT'S MY LAW I MADE IT UP!
I'LL BE GLAD WHEN THIS GAME IS OVER!
JUG, MEET THE JUG!
IT SURE IS A FULL ONE!
LET US OUT!
TIME'S UP!!
MY TURN TO BE COP!
NOW I'D LIKE TO SHOW YOU ALL A FEW MAGIC TRICKS!
GROAN!
CAN YOU DISAPPEAR?
NOW WATCH WHAT HAPPENS WHEN I DROP A COIN INTO MY HAT!

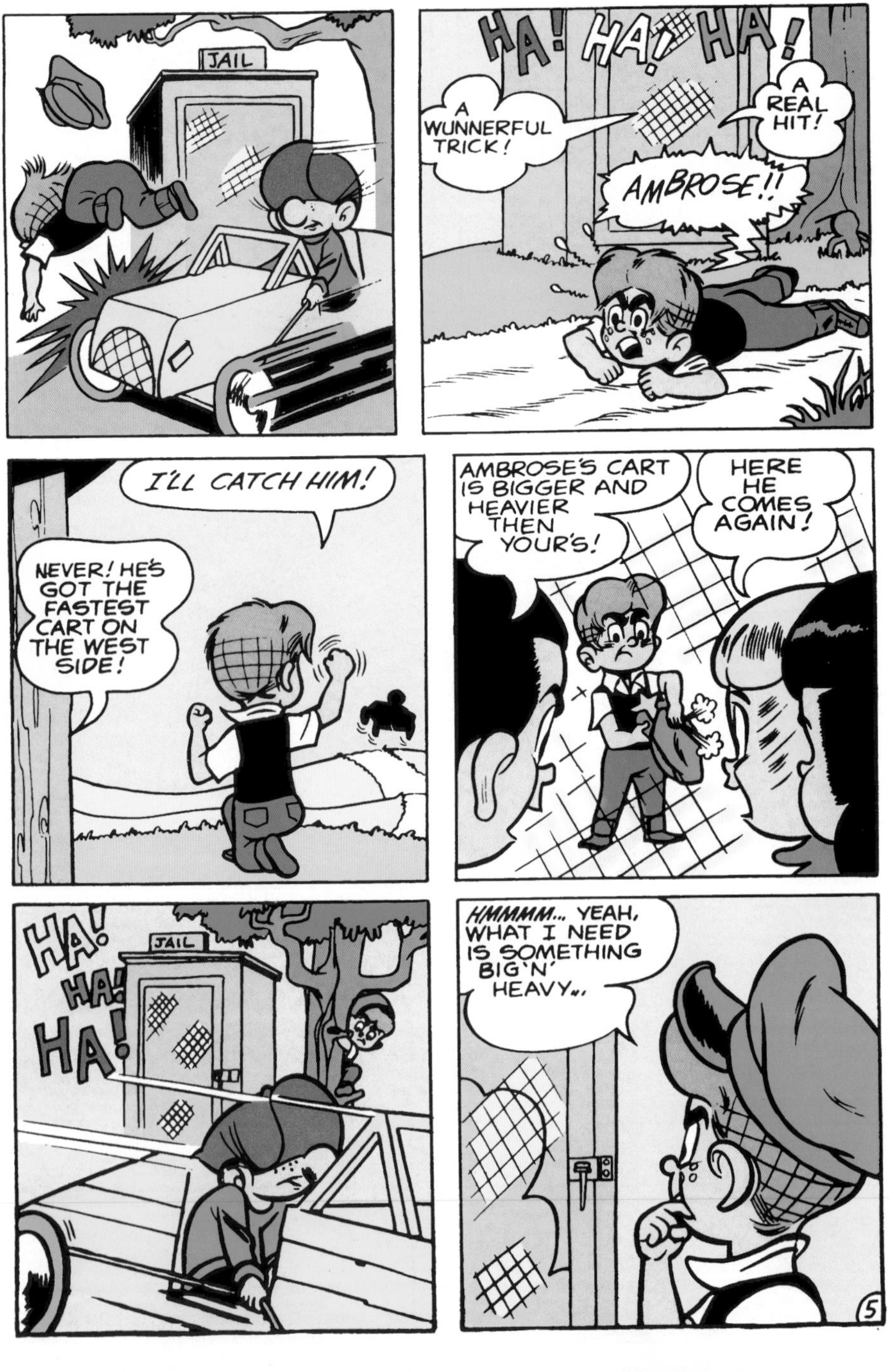
JAIL
HA! HA! HA!
A WUNNERFUL TRICK!
A REAL HIT!
AMBROSE!!
I'LL CATCH HIM!
NEVER! HE'S GOT THE FASTEST CART ON THE WEST SIDE!
AMBROSE'S CART IS BIGGER AND HEAVIER THEN YOUR'S!
HERE HE COMES AGAIN!
JAIL
HA! HA! HA!
HMMMM... YEAH, WHAT I NEED IS SOMETHING BIG'N' HEAVY..
5

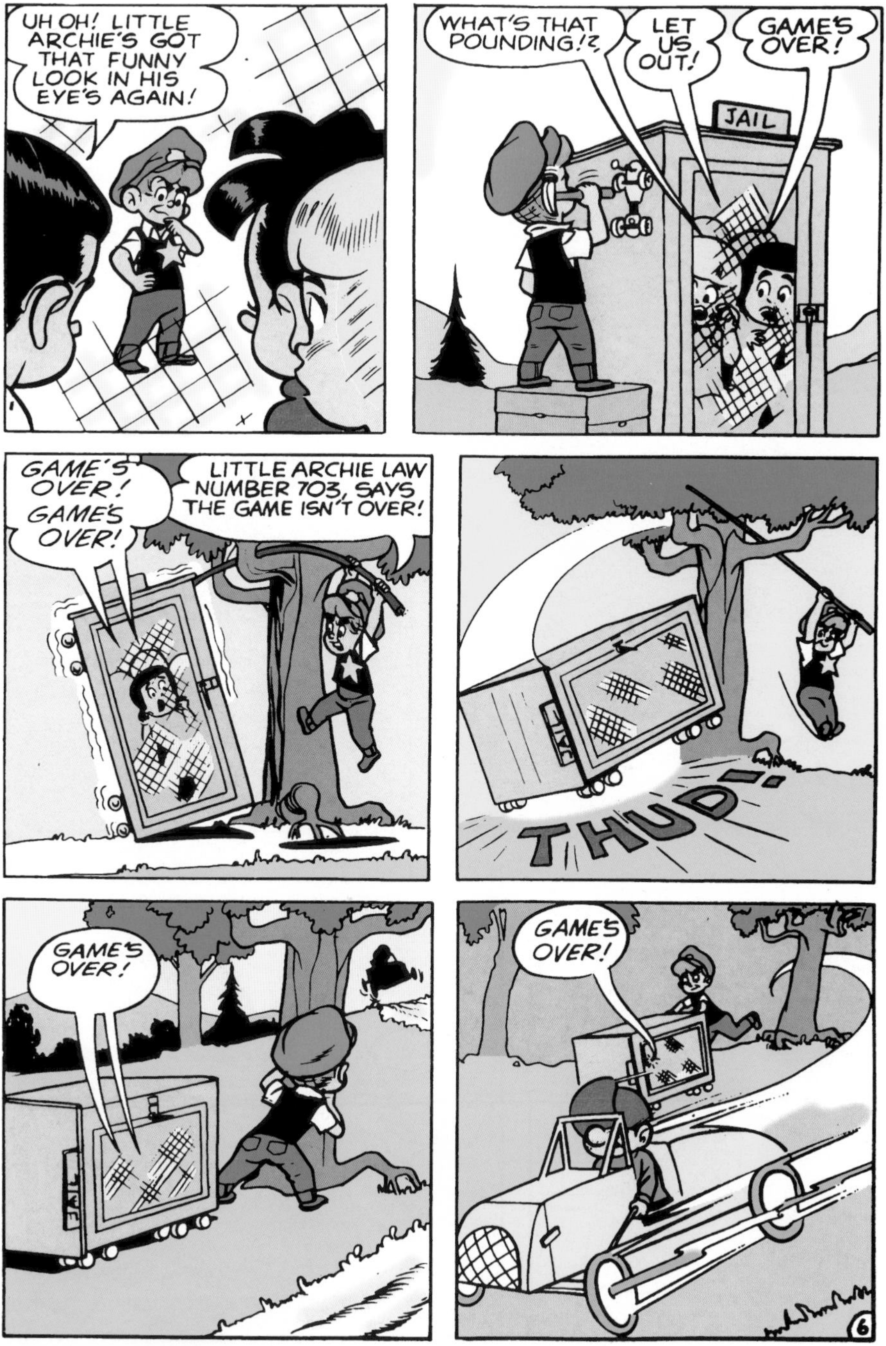
UH OH! LITTLE ARCHIE'S GOT THAT FUNNY LOOK IN HIS EYE'S AGAIN!
WHAT'S THAT POUNDING!?
LET US OUT!
GAME'S OVER!
JAIL
GAME'S OVER! GAME'S OVER!
LITTLE ARCHIE LAW NUMBER 703, SAYS THE GAME ISN'T OVER!
JAIL
THUD--
GAME'S OVER!
JAIL
GAME'S OVER!
6

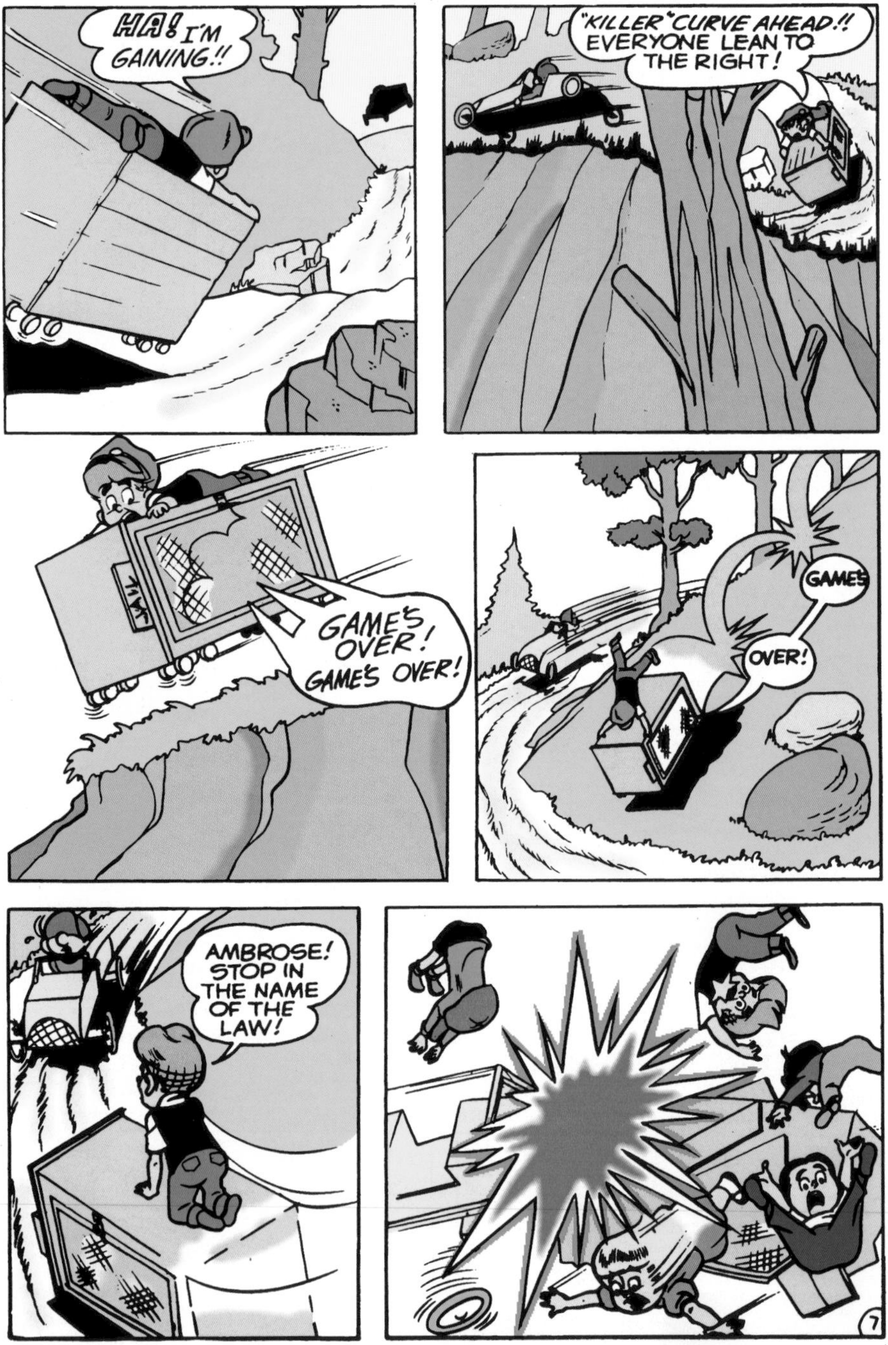
HA! I'M GAINING!!
"KILLER" CURVE AHEAD!! EVERYONE LEAN TO THE RIGHT!
GAME'S OVER! GAME'S OVER!
GAME'S
OVER!
AMBROSE! STOP IN THE NAME OF THE LAW!
7

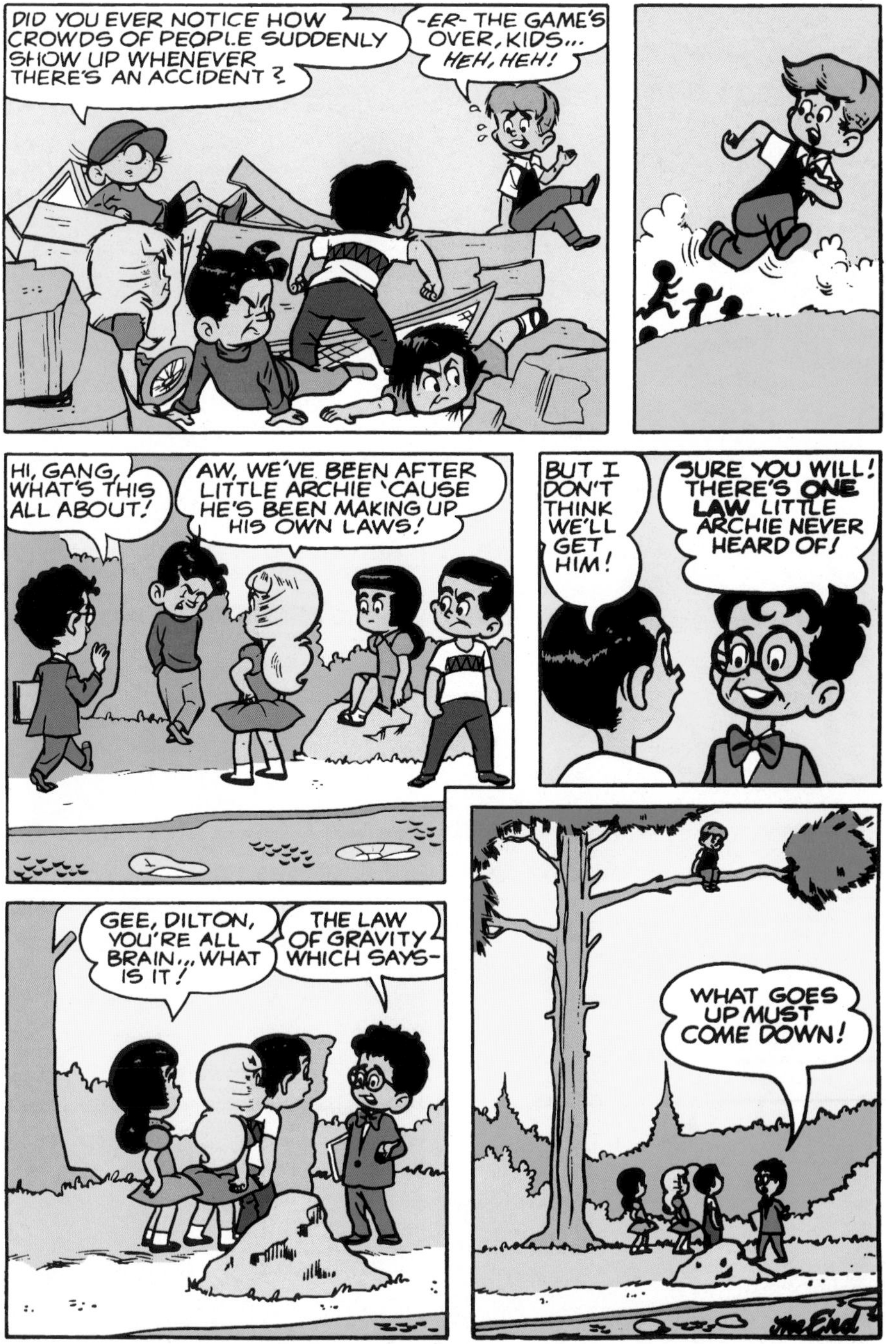
DID YOU EVER NOTICE HOW CROWDS OF PEOPLE SUDDENLY SHOW UP WHENEVER THERE'S AN ACCIDENT?
-ER- THE GAME'S OVER, KIDS... HEH, HEH!
HI, GANG, WHAT'S THIS ALL ABOUT!
AW, WE'VE BEEN AFTER LITTLE ARCHIE 'CAUSE HE'S BEEN MAKING UP HIS OWN LAWS!
BUT I DON'T THINK WE'LL GET HIM!
SURE YOU WILL! THERE'S **ONE LAW** LITTLE ARCHIE NEVER HEARD OF!
GEE, DILTON, YOU'RE ALL BRAIN... WHAT IS IT!
THE LAW OF GRAVITY WHICH SAYS-
WHAT GOES UP MUST COME DOWN!
The End

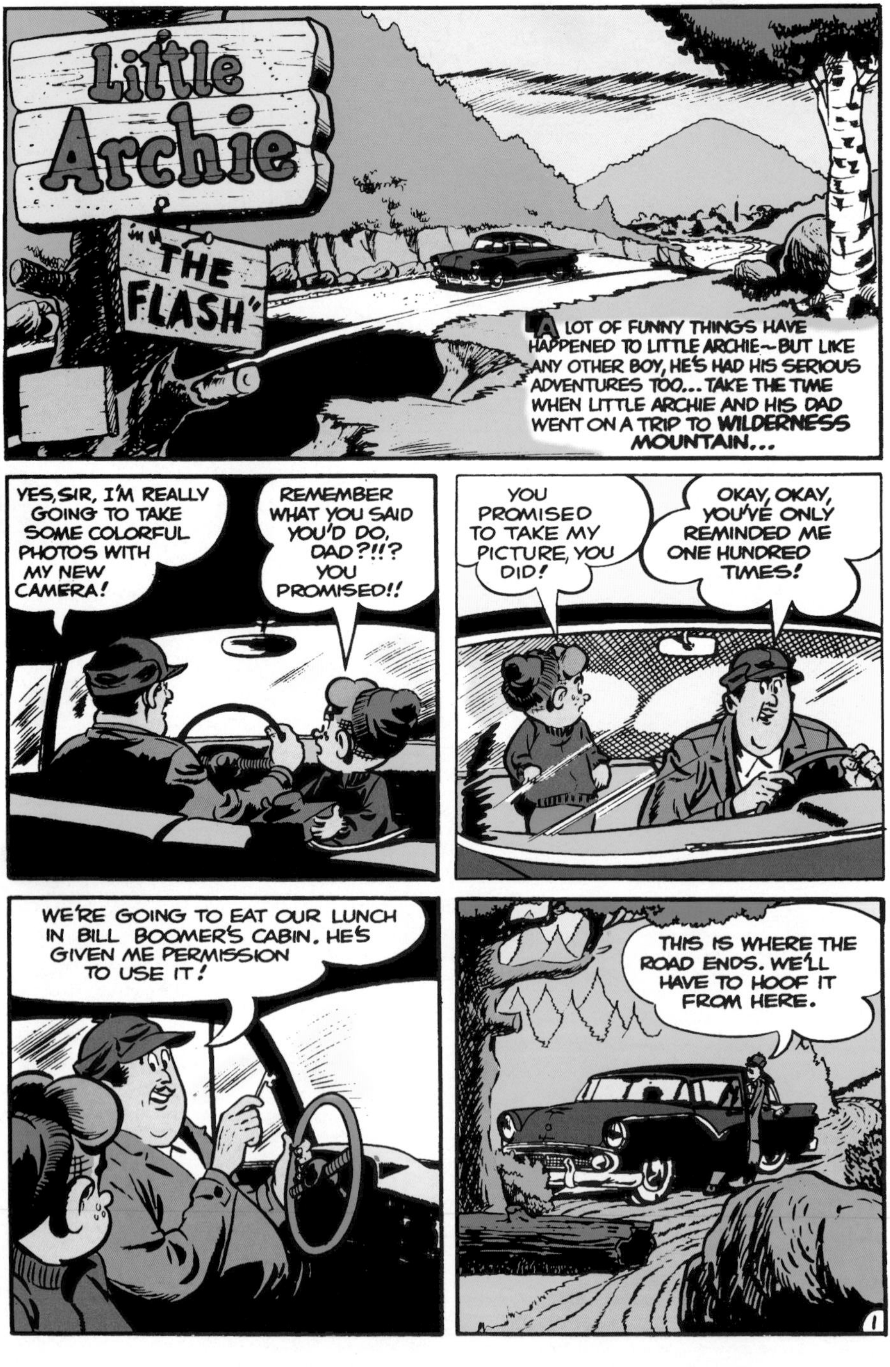
Little Archie
in "THE FLASH"
A LOT OF FUNNY THINGS HAVE HAPPENED TO LITTLE ARCHIE~BUT LIKE ANY OTHER BOY, HE'S HAD HIS SERIOUS ADVENTURES TOO... TAKE THE TIME WHEN LITTLE ARCHIE AND HIS DAD WENT ON A TRIP TO WILDERNESS MOUNTAIN...
YES,SIR, I'M REALLY GOING TO TAKE SOME COLORFUL PHOTOS WITH MY NEW CAMERA!
REMEMBER WHAT YOU SAID YOU'D DO, DAD?!!? YOU PROMISED!!
YOU PROMISED TO TAKE MY PICTURE, YOU DID!
OKAY, OKAY, YOU'VE ONLY REMINDED ME ONE HUNDRED TIMES!
WE'RE GOING TO EAT OUR LUNCH IN BILL BOOMER'S CABIN. HE'S GIVEN ME PERMISSION TO USE IT!
THIS IS WHERE THE ROAD ENDS. WE'LL HAVE TO HOOF IT FROM HERE.
1

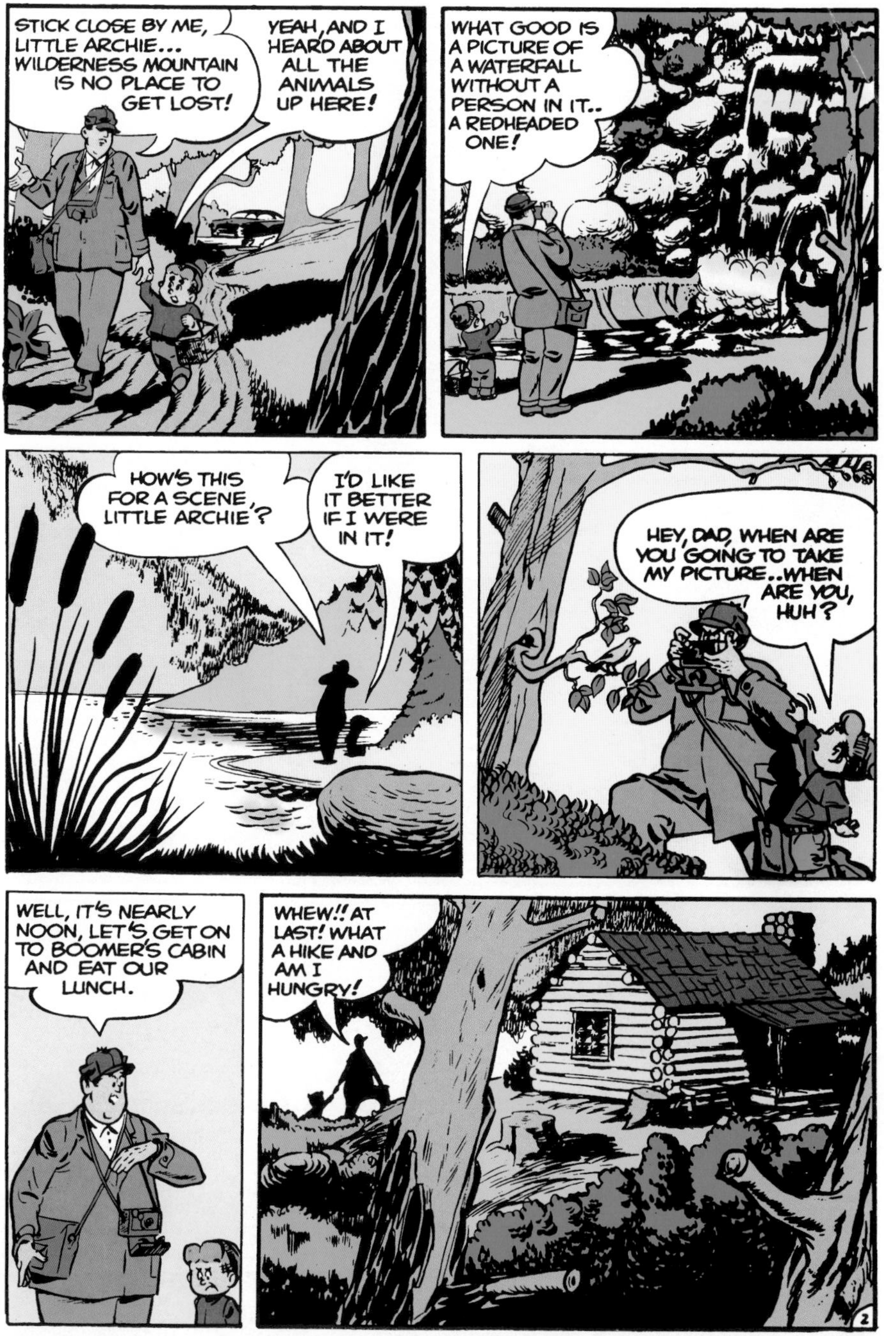
STICK CLOSE BY ME, LITTLE ARCHIE... WILDERNESS MOUNTAIN IS NO PLACE TO GET LOST!
YEAH, AND I HEARD ABOUT ALL THE ANIMALS UP HERE!
WHAT GOOD IS A PICTURE OF A WATERFALL WITHOUT A PERSON IN IT.. A REDHEADED ONE!
HOW'S THIS FOR A SCENE, LITTLE ARCHIE?
I'D LIKE IT BETTER IF I WERE IN IT!
HEY, DAD, WHEN ARE YOU GOING TO TAKE MY PICTURE..WHEN ARE YOU, HUH?
WELL, IT'S NEARLY NOON, LET'S GET ON TO BOOMER'S CABIN AND EAT OUR LUNCH.
WHEW!! AT LAST! WHAT A HIKE AND AM I HUNGRY!
2

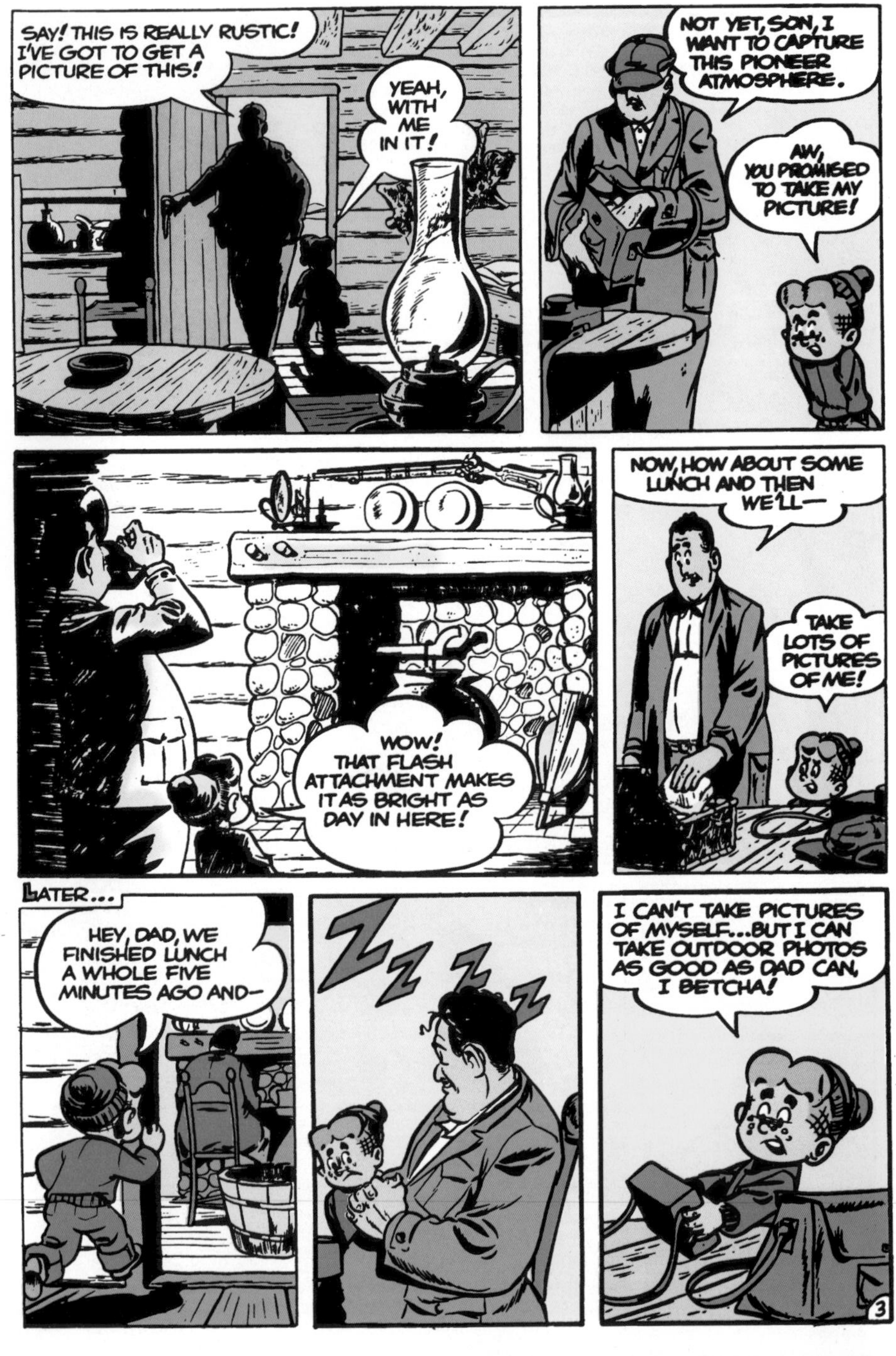
SAY! THIS IS REALLY RUSTIC! I'VE GOT TO GET A PICTURE OF THIS!
YEAH, WITH ME IN IT!
NOT YET, SON, I WANT TO CAPTURE THIS PIONEER ATMOSPHERE.
AW, YOU PROMISED TO TAKE MY PICTURE!
WOW! THAT FLASH ATTACHMENT MAKES IT AS BRIGHT AS DAY IN HERE!
NOW, HOW ABOUT SOME LUNCH AND THEN WE'LL—
TAKE LOTS OF PICTURES OF ME!
LATER...
HEY, DAD, WE FINISHED LUNCH A WHOLE FIVE MINUTES AGO AND—
Z Z Z Z
I CAN'T TAKE PICTURES OF MYSELF...BUT I CAN TAKE OUTDOOR PHOTOS AS GOOD AS DAD CAN, I BETCHA!
3

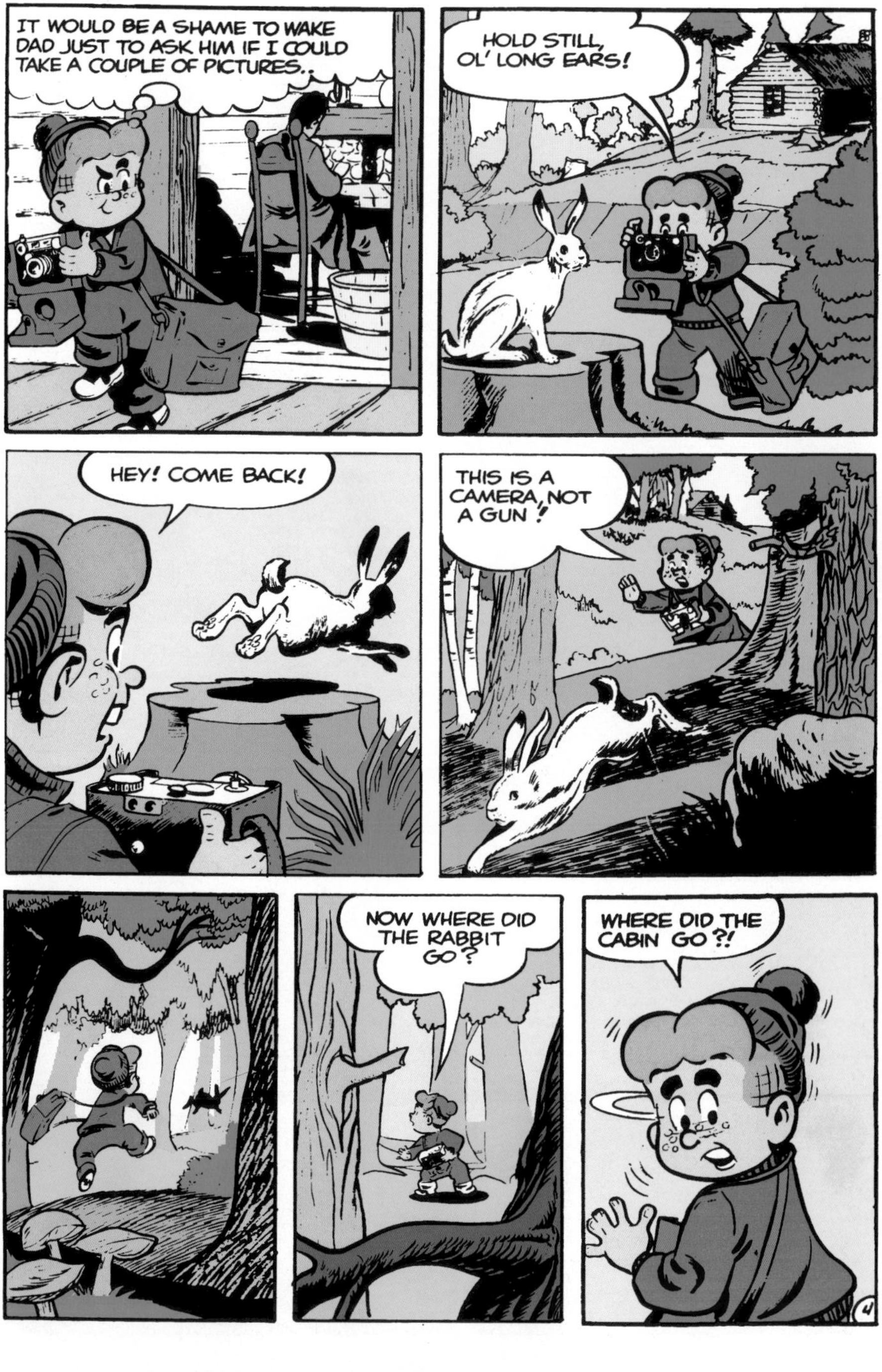
IT WOULD BE A SHAME TO WAKE DAD JUST TO ASK HIM IF I COULD TAKE A COUPLE OF PICTURES..
HOLD STILL, OL' LONG EARS!
HEY! COME BACK!
THIS IS A CAMERA, NOT A GUN!
NOW WHERE DID THE RABBIT GO?
WHERE DID THE CABIN GO?!
4

GOLLY! THIS ISN'T THE WAY BACK!

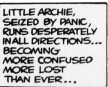

LITTLE ARCHIE, SEIZED BY PANIC, RUNS DESPERATELY IN ALL DIRECTIONS... BECOMING MORE CONFUSED MORE LOST THAN EVER...

"SOB" I-I'M LOST!

A STREAM! ONE TIME A BOY SCOUT TOLD ME THAT IF I EVER GOT LOST TO WALK DOWN STREAM!

GOSH, I'VE BEEN GOING DOWN STREAM FOR A LONG TIME AND IT'S GONNA GET DARK SOON AND—

5

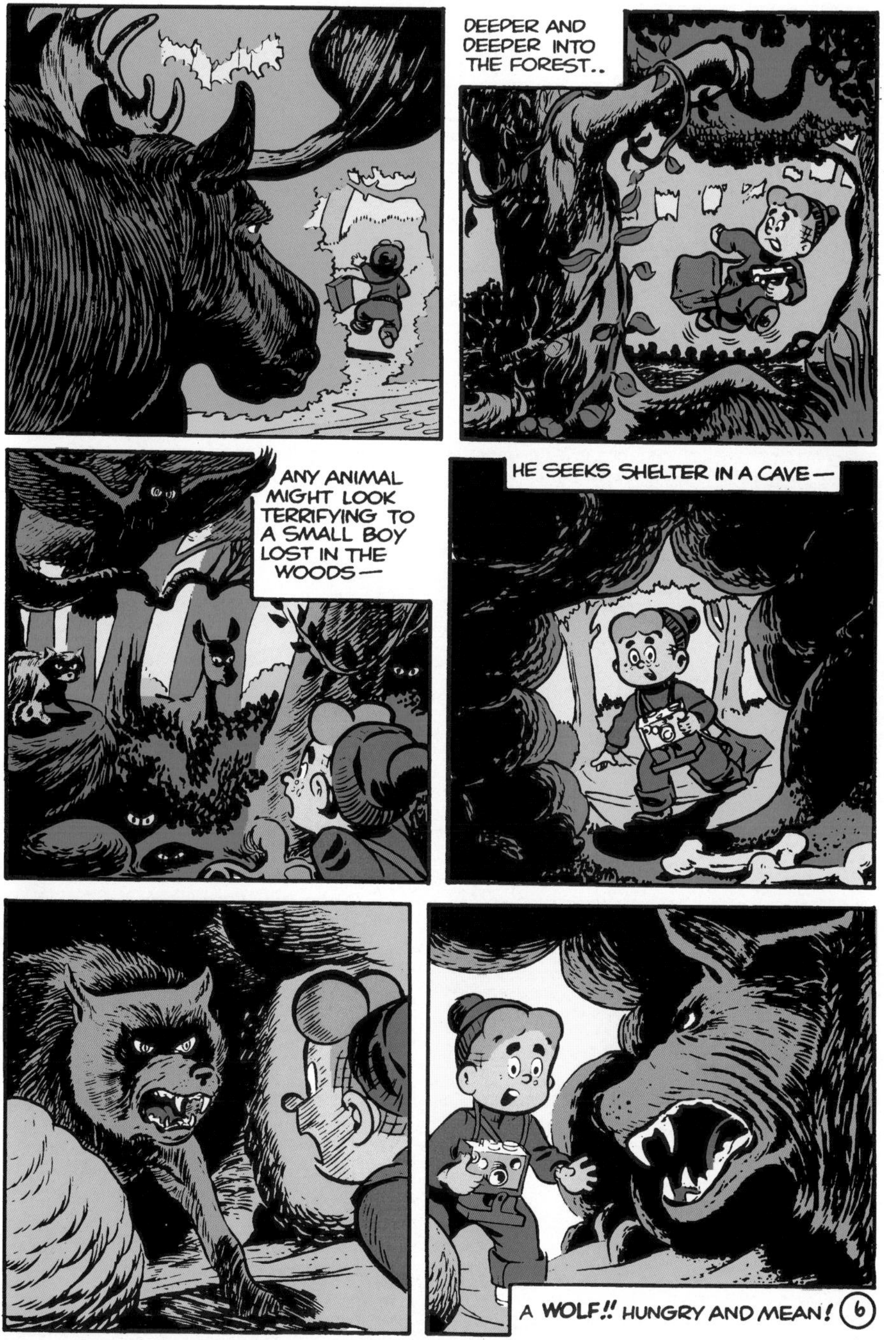
DEEPER AND DEEPER INTO THE FOREST..
ANY ANIMAL MIGHT LOOK TERRIFYING TO A SMALL BOY LOST IN THE WOODS—
HE SEEKS SHELTER IN A CAVE—
A WOLF!! HUNGRY AND MEAN!
6

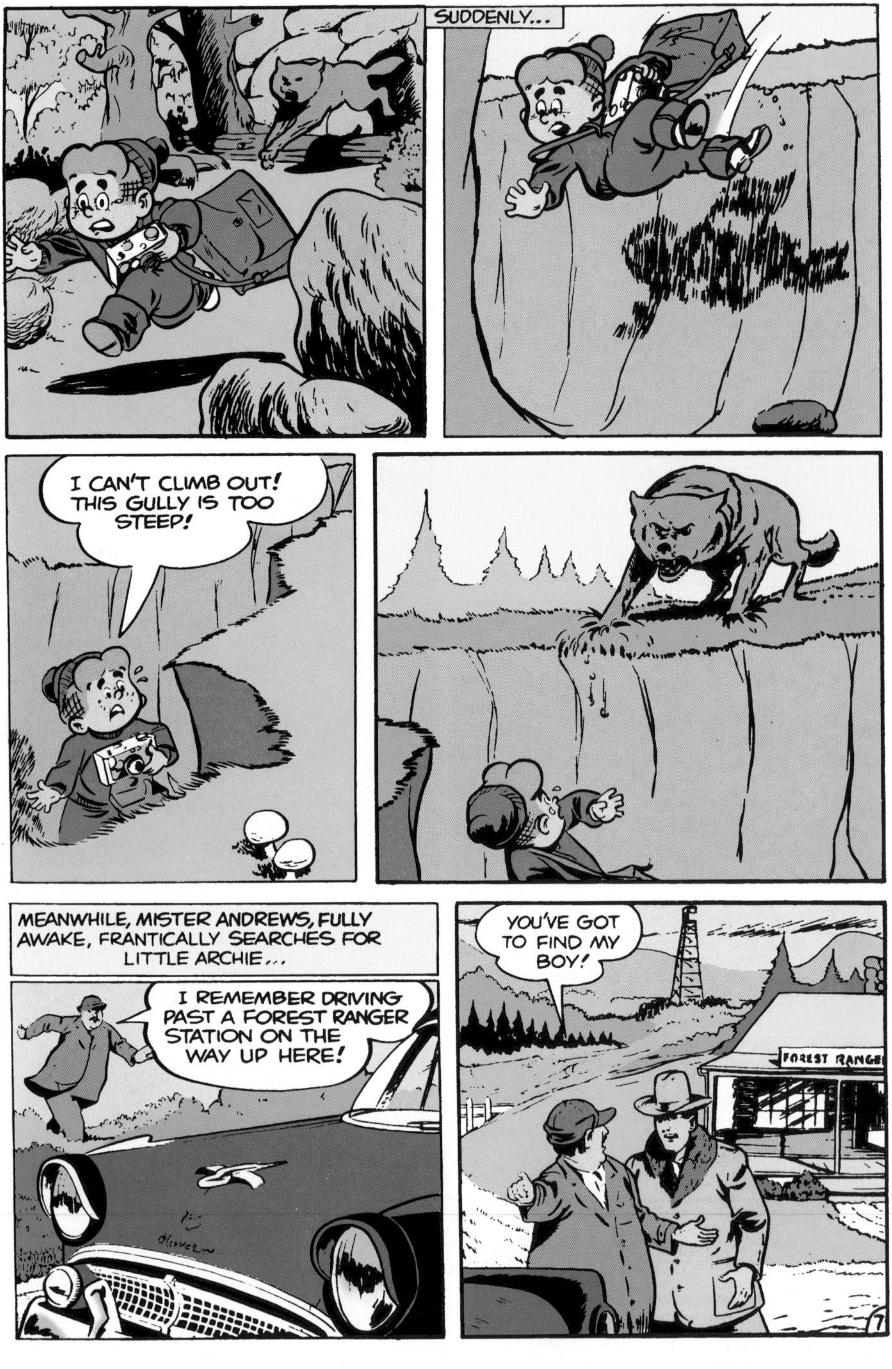
SUDDENLY...
I CAN'T CLIMB OUT! THIS GULLY IS TOO STEEP!
MEANWHILE, MISTER ANDREWS, FULLY AWAKE, FRANTICALLY SEARCHES FOR LITTLE ARCHIE...
I REMEMBER DRIVING PAST A FOREST RANGER STATION ON THE WAY UP HERE!
YOU'VE GOT TO FIND MY BOY!
FOREST RANGE
7

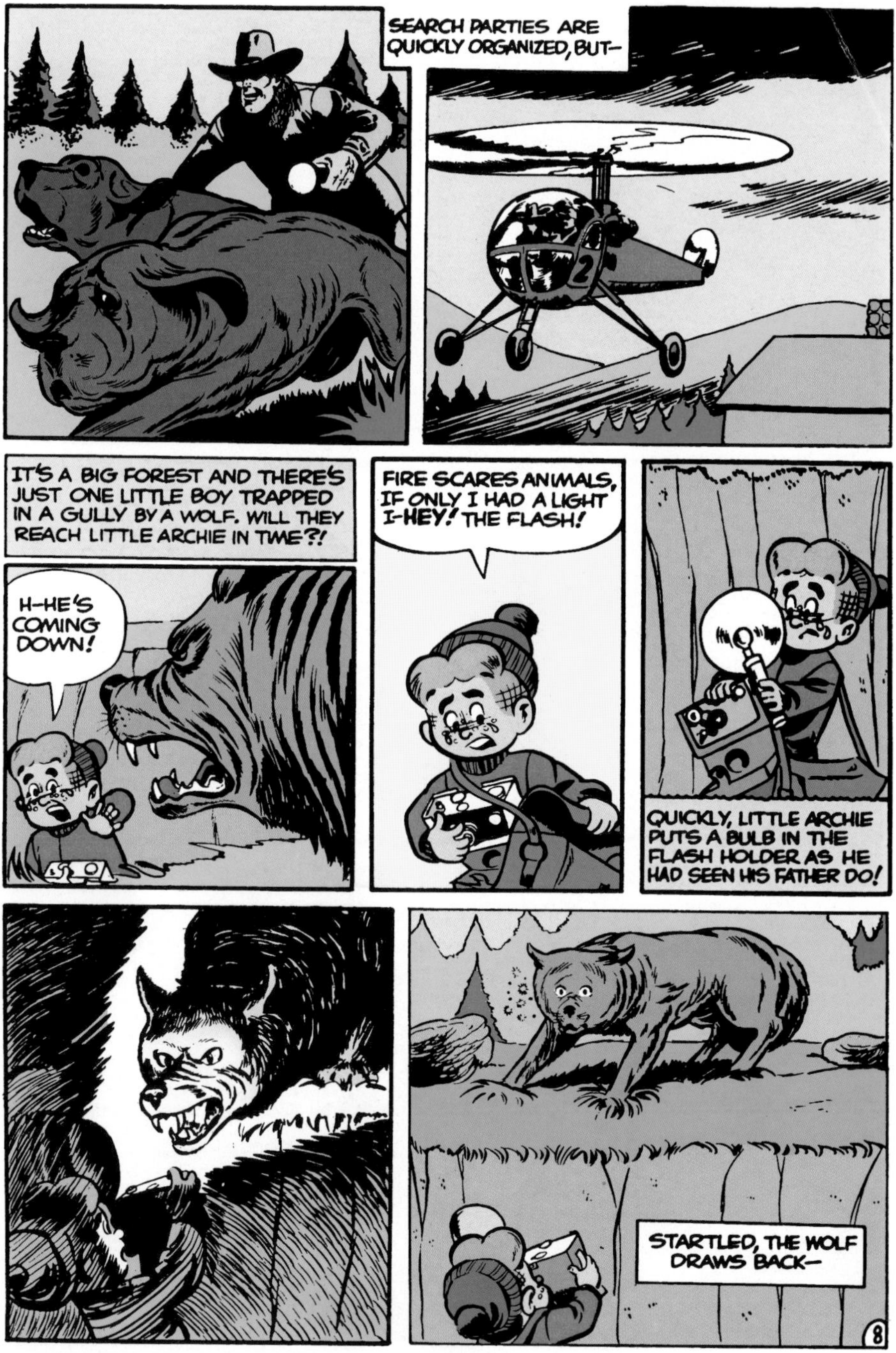
SEARCH PARTIES ARE QUICKLY ORGANIZED, BUT—
2
IT'S A BIG FOREST AND THERE'S JUST ONE LITTLE BOY TRAPPED IN A GULLY BY A WOLF. WILL THEY REACH LITTLE ARCHIE IN TIME?!
H-HE'S COMING DOWN!
FIRE SCARES ANIMALS, IF ONLY I HAD A LIGHT I-HEY! THE FLASH!
QUICKLY, LITTLE ARCHIE PUTS A BULB IN THE FLASH HOLDER AS HE HAD SEEN HIS FATHER DO!
STARTLED, THE WOLF DRAWS BACK—
8

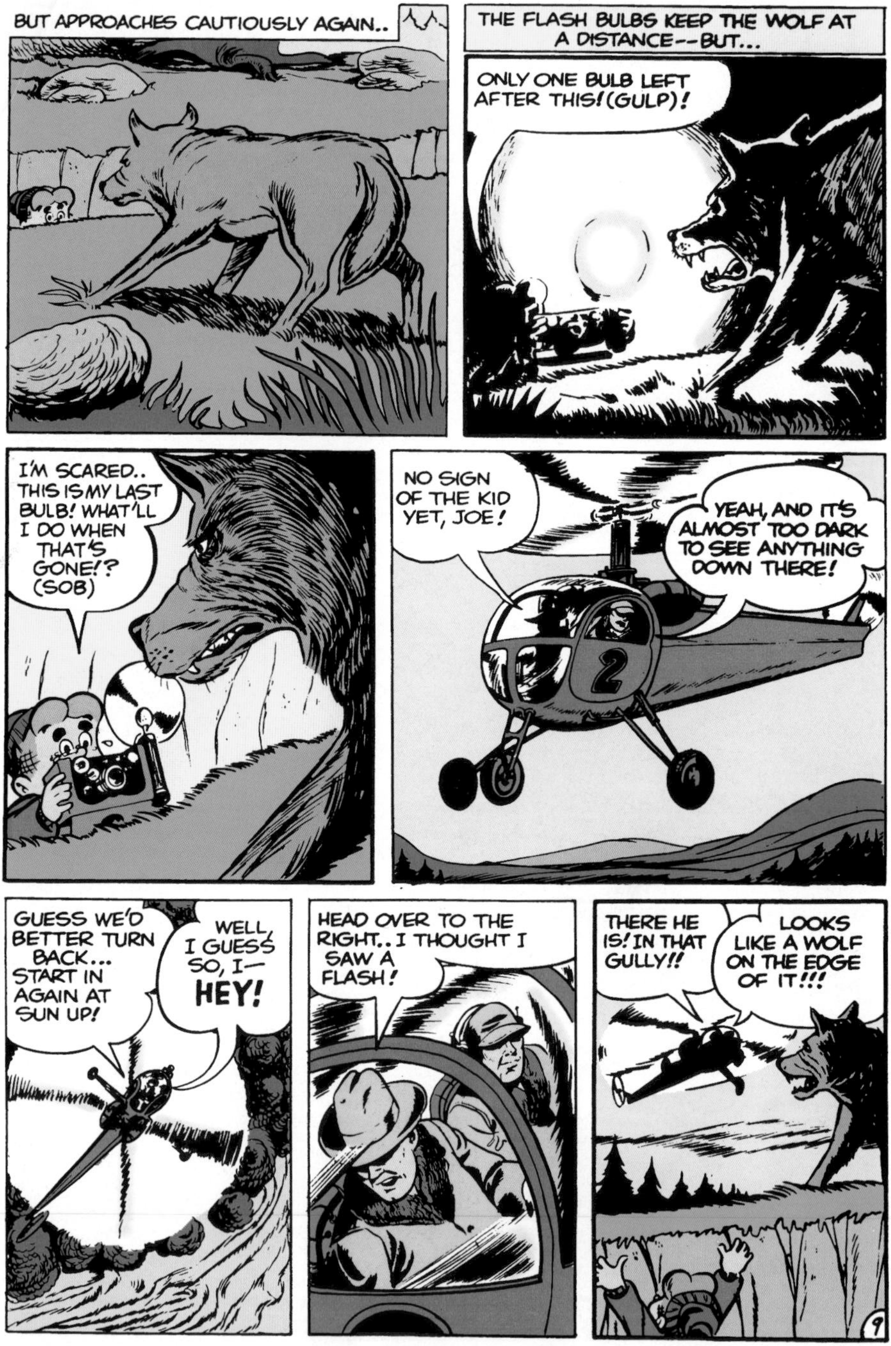
BUT APPROACHES CAUTIOUSLY AGAIN..
THE FLASH BULBS KEEP THE WOLF AT A DISTANCE--BUT...
ONLY ONE BULB LEFT AFTER THIS! (GULP)!
I'M SCARED.. THIS IS MY LAST BULB! WHAT'LL I DO WHEN THAT'S GONE!? (SOB)
NO SIGN OF THE KID YET, JOE!
YEAH, AND IT'S ALMOST TOO DARK TO SEE ANYTHING DOWN THERE!
2
GUESS WE'D BETTER TURN BACK... START IN AGAIN AT SUN UP!
WELL, I GUESS SO, I— HEY!
HEAD OVER TO THE RIGHT.. I THOUGHT I SAW A FLASH!
THERE HE IS! IN THAT GULLY!!
LOOKS LIKE A WOLF ON THE EDGE OF IT!!!
9

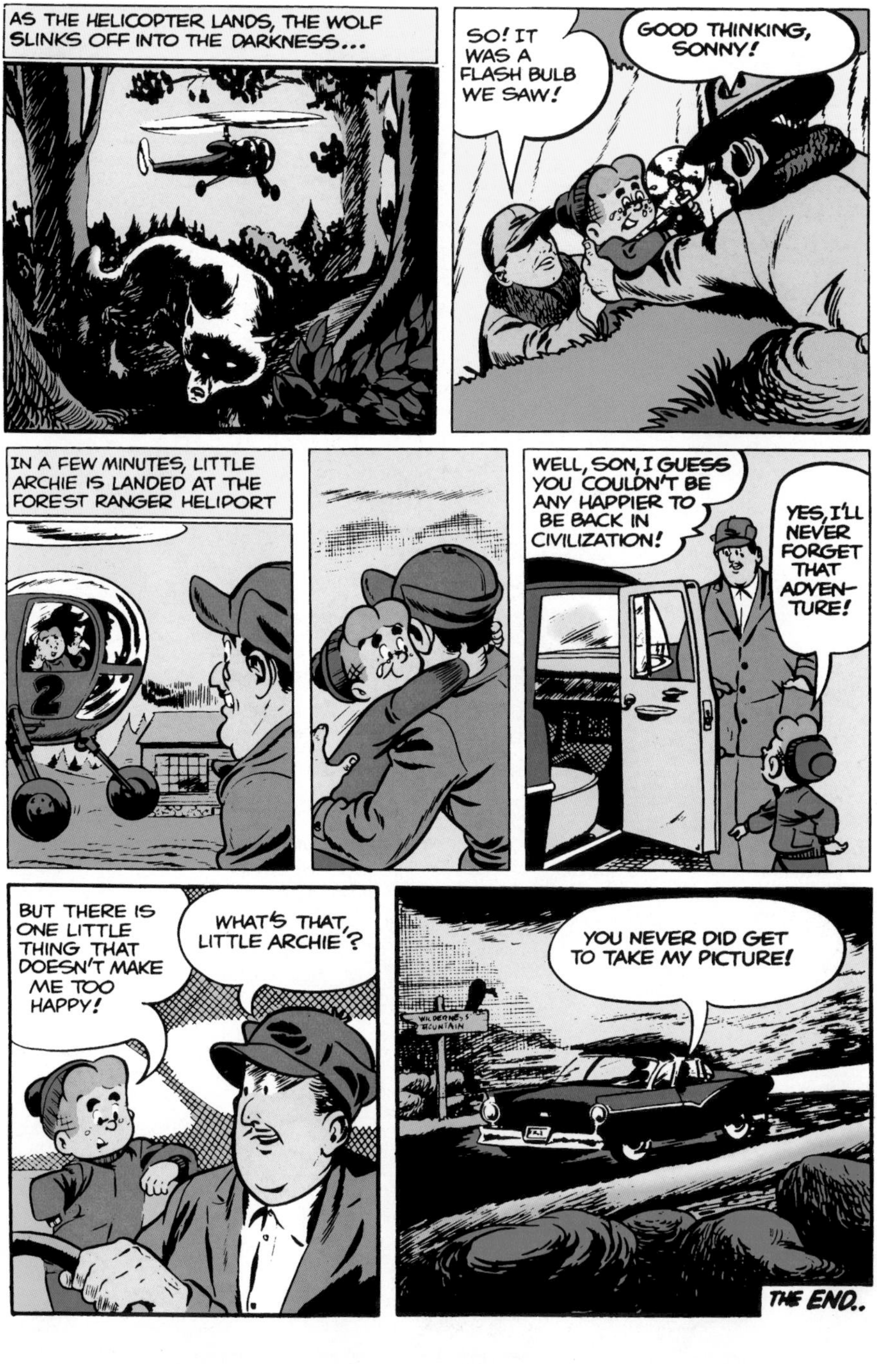
AS THE HELICOPTER LANDS, THE WOLF SLINKS OFF INTO THE DARKNESS...
SO! IT WAS A FLASH BULB WE SAW!
GOOD THINKING, SONNY!
IN A FEW MINUTES, LITTLE ARCHIE IS LANDED AT THE FOREST RANGER HELIPORT
2
WELL, SON, I GUESS YOU COULDN'T BE ANY HAPPIER TO BE BACK IN CIVILIZATION!
YES, I'LL NEVER FORGET THAT ADVEN-TURE!
BUT THERE IS ONE LITTLE THING THAT DOESN'T MAKE ME TOO HAPPY!
WHAT'S THAT, LITTLE ARCHIE?
YOU NEVER DID GET TO TAKE MY PICTURE!
THE END..

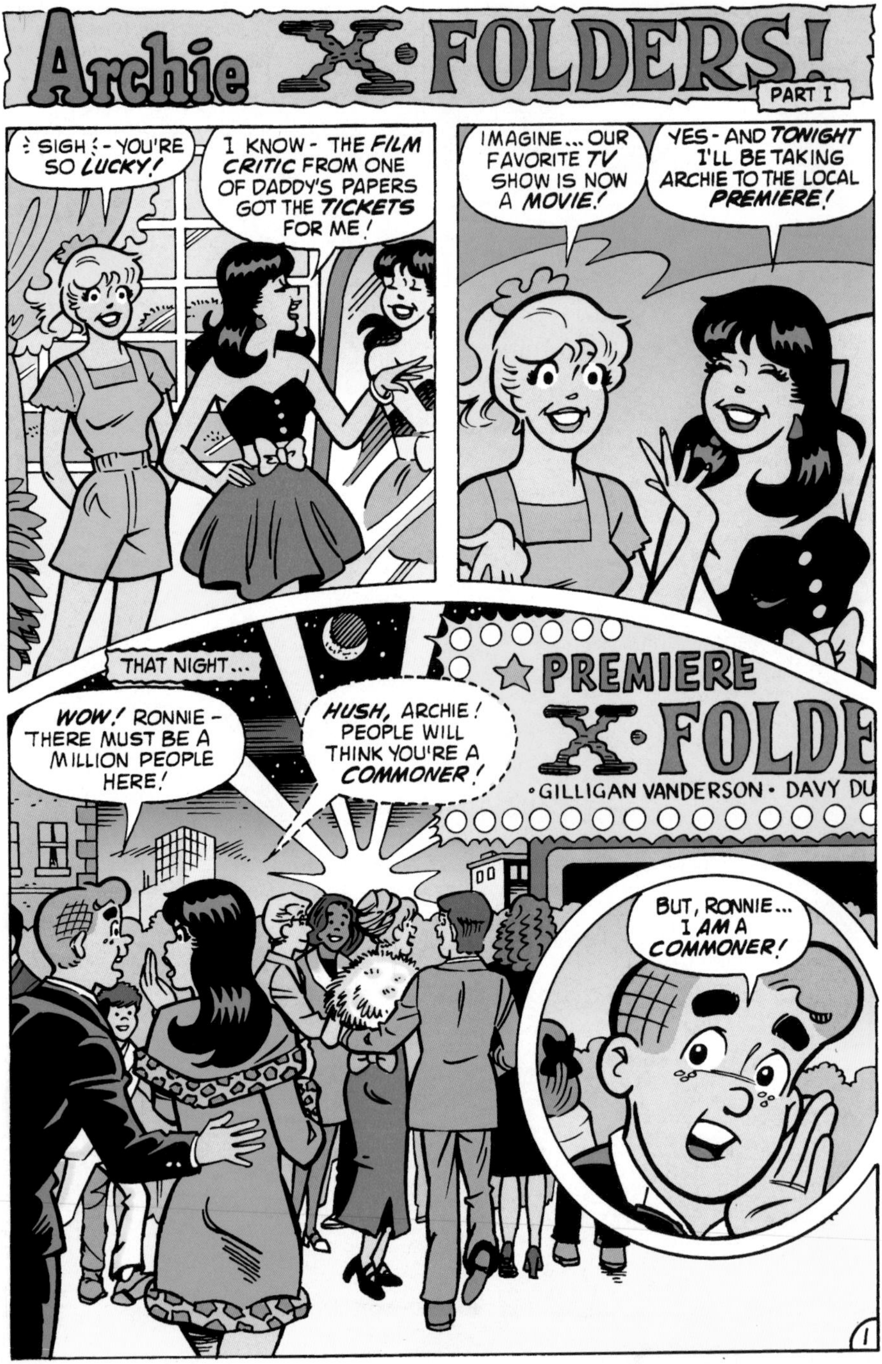
Archie X-FOLDERS!
PART I
:SIGH: - YOU'RE SO LUCKY!
I KNOW - THE FILM CRITIC FROM ONE OF DADDY'S PAPERS GOT THE TICKETS FOR ME!
IMAGINE... OUR FAVORITE TV SHOW IS NOW A MOVIE!
YES - AND TONIGHT I'LL BE TAKING ARCHIE TO THE LOCAL PREMIERE!
THAT NIGHT...
PREMIERE
X-FOLDE
•GILLIGAN VANDERSON • DAVY DU
WOW! RONNIE - THERE MUST BE A MILLION PEOPLE HERE!
HUSH, ARCHIE! PEOPLE WILL THINK YOU'RE A COMMONER!
BUT, RONNIE... I AM A COMMONER!
1

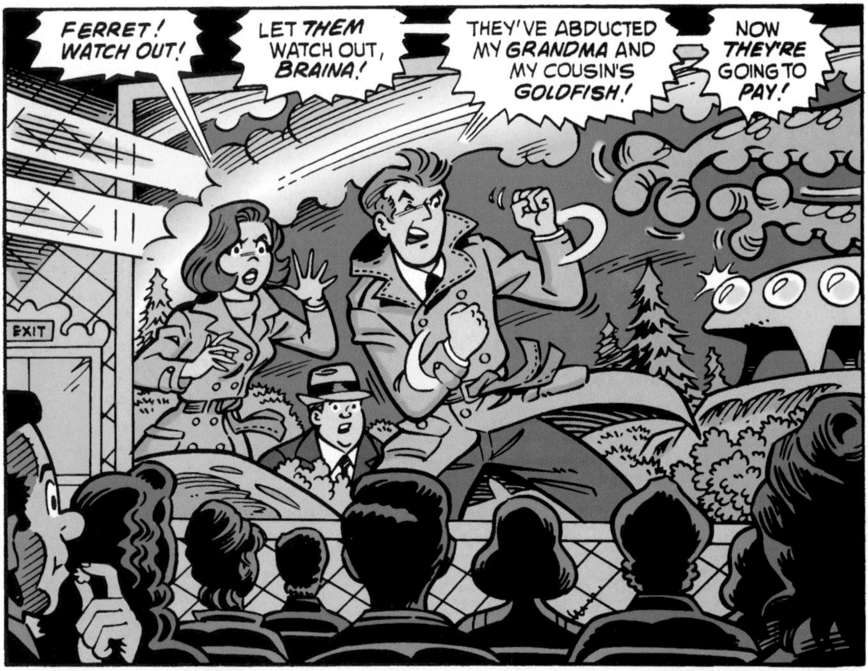
FERRET! WATCH OUT!
LET THEM WATCH OUT, BRAINA!
THEY'VE ABDUCTED MY GRANDMA AND MY COUSIN'S GOLDFISH!
NOW THEY'RE GOING TO PAY!
EXIT

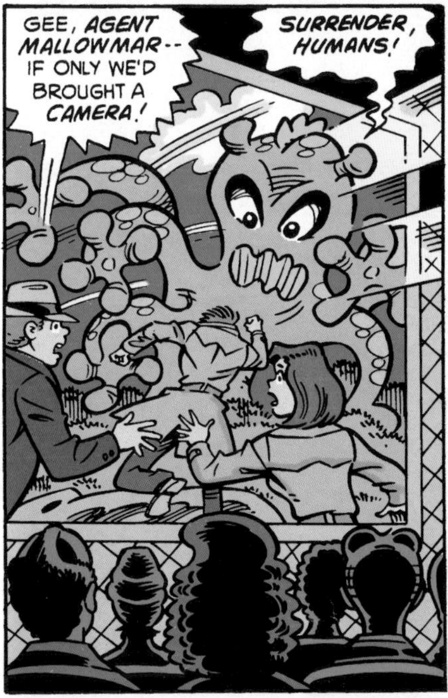
GEE, AGENT MALLOWMAR-- IF ONLY WE'D BROUGHT A CAMERA!
SURRENDER, HUMANS!

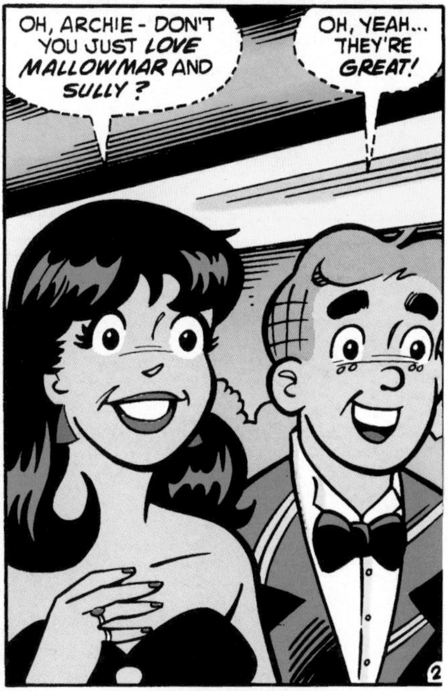
OH, ARCHIE - DON'T YOU JUST LOVE MALLOWMAR AND SULLY?
OH, YEAH... THEY'RE GREAT!
2

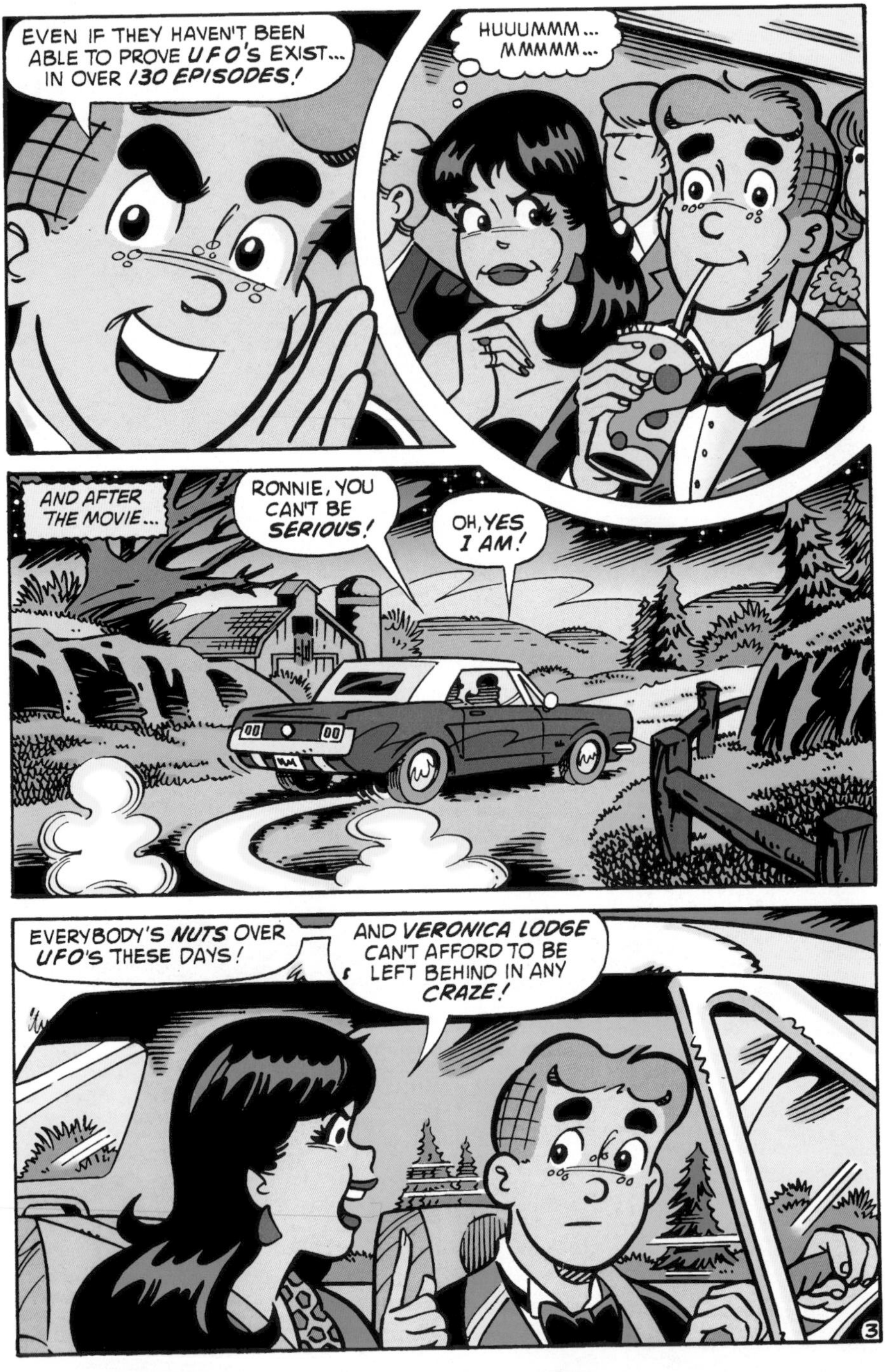
EVEN IF THEY HAVEN'T BEEN ABLE TO PROVE UFO'S EXIST... IN OVER 130 EPISODES!
HUUUMMM... MMMMM...
AND AFTER THE MOVIE...
RONNIE, YOU CAN'T BE SERIOUS!
OH, YES I AM!
EVERYBODY'S NUTS OVER UFO'S THESE DAYS!
AND VERONICA LODGE CAN'T AFFORD TO BE LEFT BEHIND IN ANY CRAZE!
3

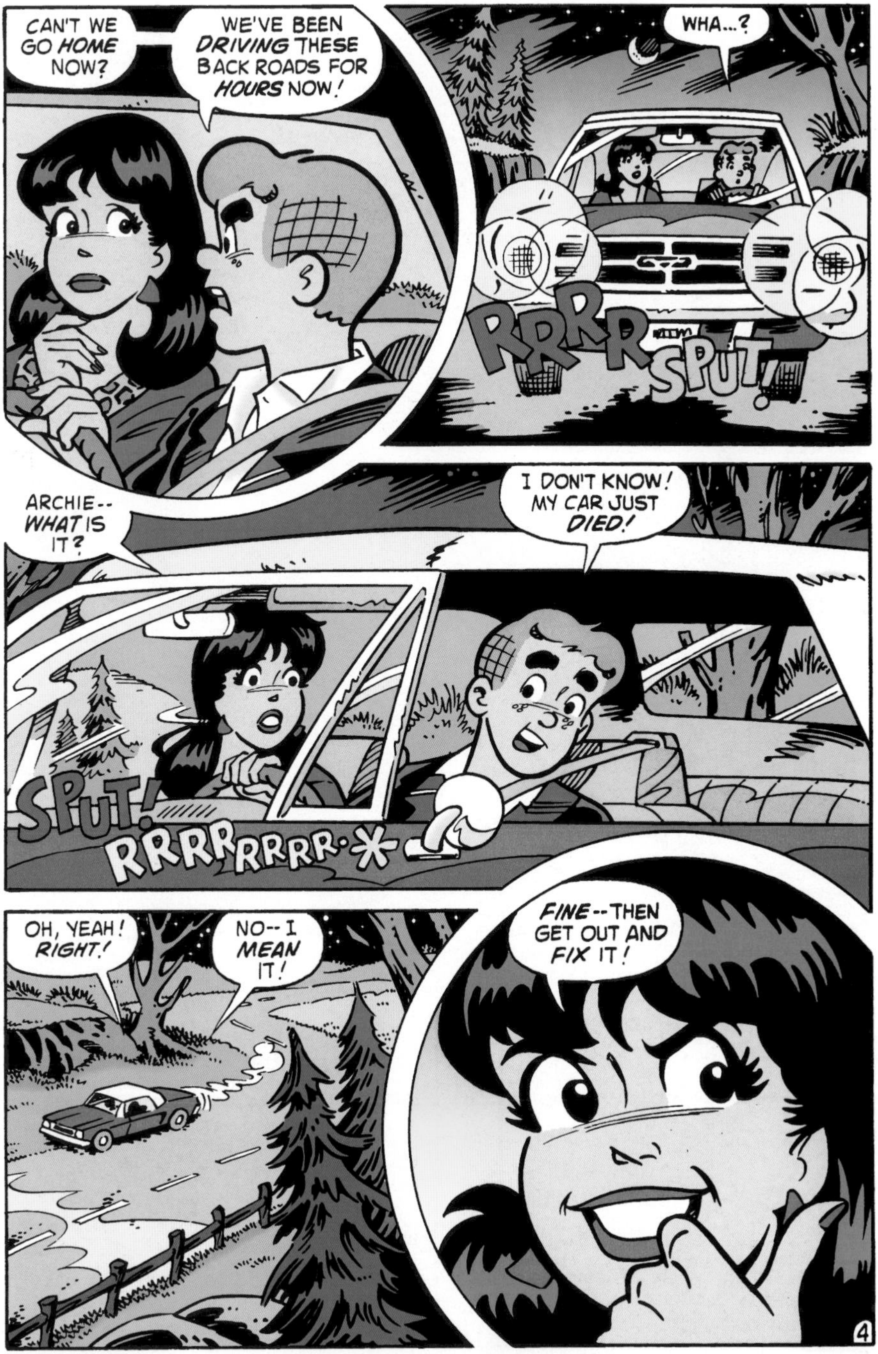
CAN'T WE GO HOME NOW?
WE'VE BEEN DRIVING THESE BACK ROADS FOR HOURS NOW!
WHA...?
RRRR SPUT!
ARCHIE-- WHAT IS IT?
I DON'T KNOW! MY CAR JUST DIED!
SPUT! RRRRRRRR·*
OH, YEAH! RIGHT!
NO-- I MEAN IT!
FINE--THEN GET OUT AND FIX IT!
4

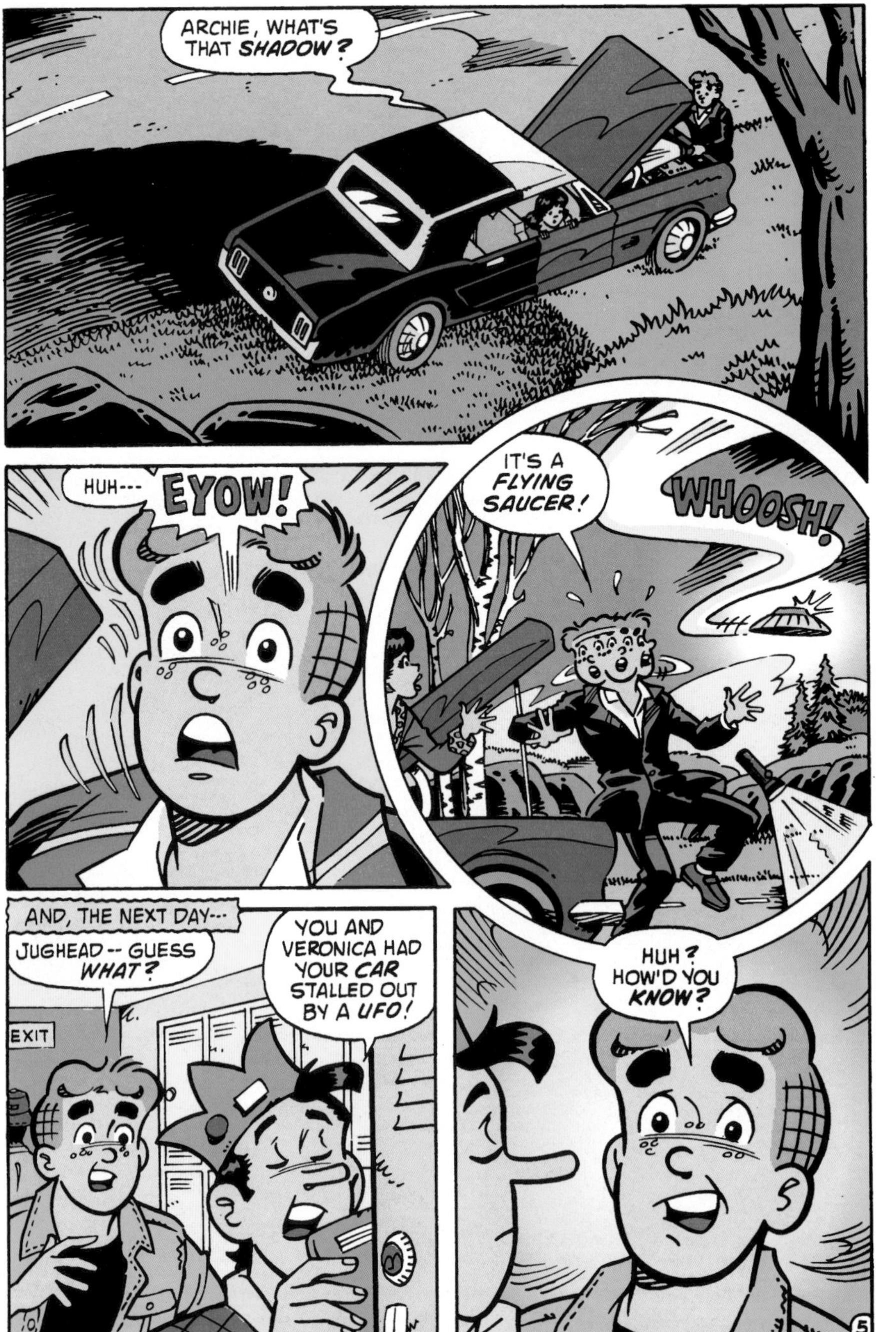
ARCHIE, WHAT'S THAT SHADOW?
HUH--- EYOW!
IT'S A FLYING SAUCER!
WHOOSH!
AND, THE NEXT DAY---
JUGHEAD -- GUESS WHAT?
EXIT
YOU AND VERONICA HAD YOUR CAR STALLED OUT BY A UFO!
HUH? HOW'D YOU KNOW?
5

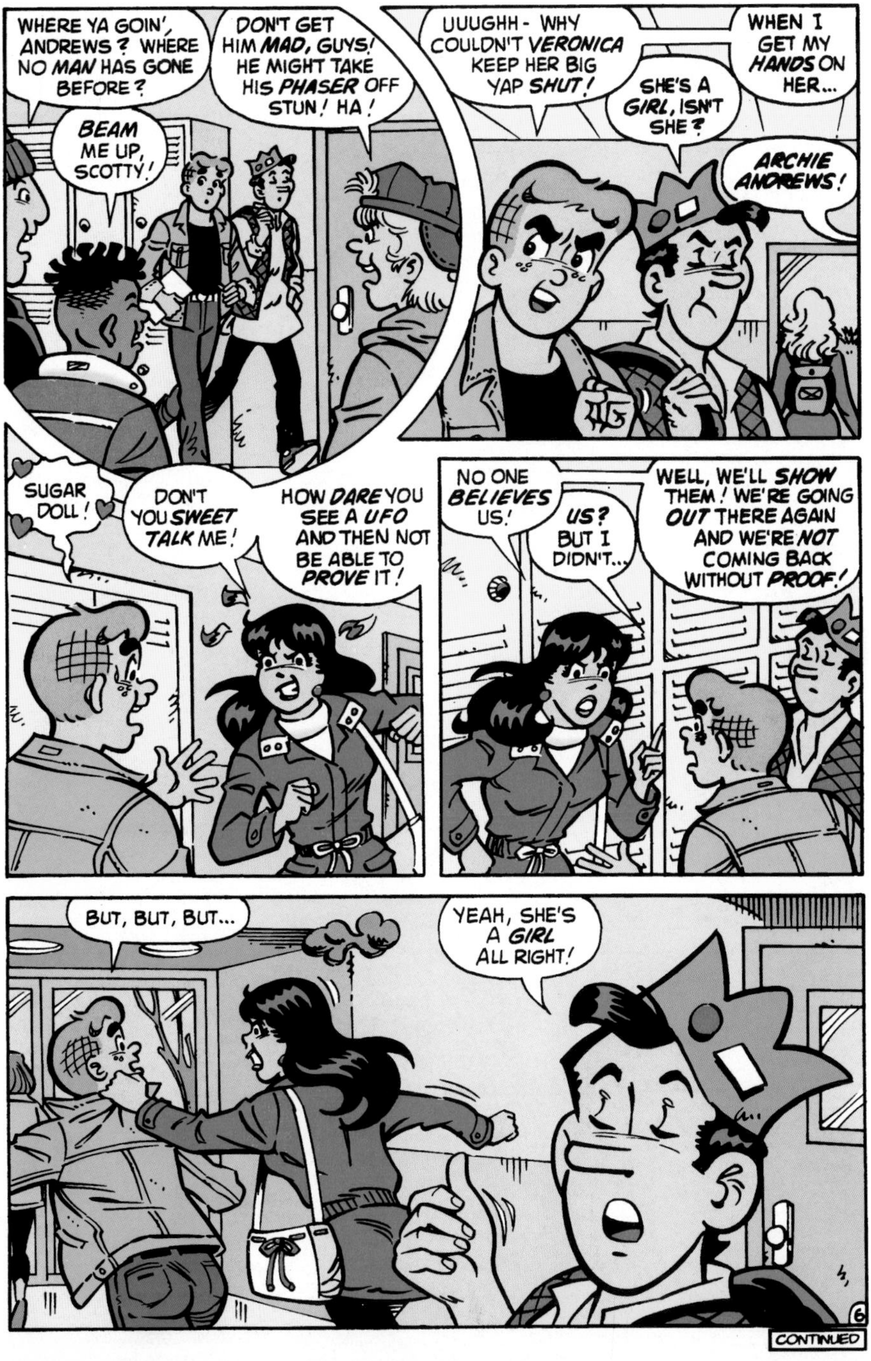
WHERE YA GOIN', ANDREWS? WHERE NO MAN HAS GONE BEFORE?
DON'T GET HIM MAD, GUYS! HE MIGHT TAKE HIS PHASER OFF STUN! HA!
BEAM ME UP, SCOTTY!
UUUGHH - WHY COULDN'T VERONICA KEEP HER BIG YAP SHUT!
WHEN I GET MY HANDS ON HER...
SHE'S A GIRL, ISN'T SHE?
ARCHIE ANDREWS!
SUGAR DOLL!
DON'T YOU SWEET TALK ME!
HOW DARE YOU SEE A UFO AND THEN NOT BE ABLE TO PROVE IT!
NO ONE BELIEVES US!
US? BUT I DIDN'T...
WELL, WE'LL SHOW THEM! WE'RE GOING OUT THERE AGAIN AND WE'RE NOT COMING BACK WITHOUT PROOF!
BUT, BUT, BUT...
YEAH, SHE'S A GIRL ALL RIGHT!
6
CONTINUED

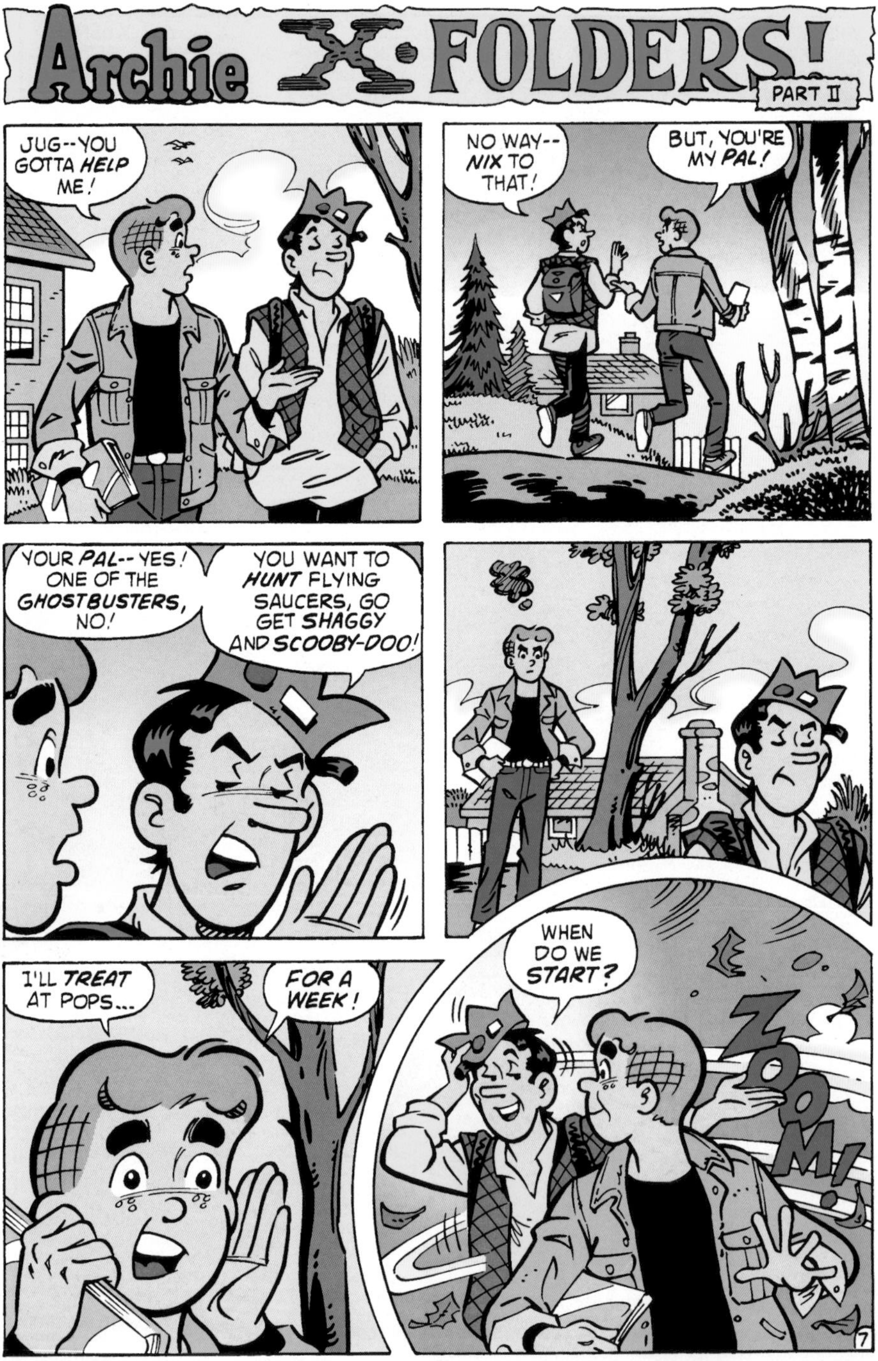
Archie X-FOLDERS!
PART II
JUG--YOU GOTTA HELP ME!
NO WAY-- NIX TO THAT!
BUT, YOU'RE MY PAL!
YOUR PAL-- YES! ONE OF THE GHOSTBUSTERS, NO!
YOU WANT TO HUNT FLYING SAUCERS, GO GET SHAGGY AND SCOOBY-DOO!
I'LL TREAT AT POPS...
FOR A WEEK!
WHEN DO WE START?
ZOOM!
7

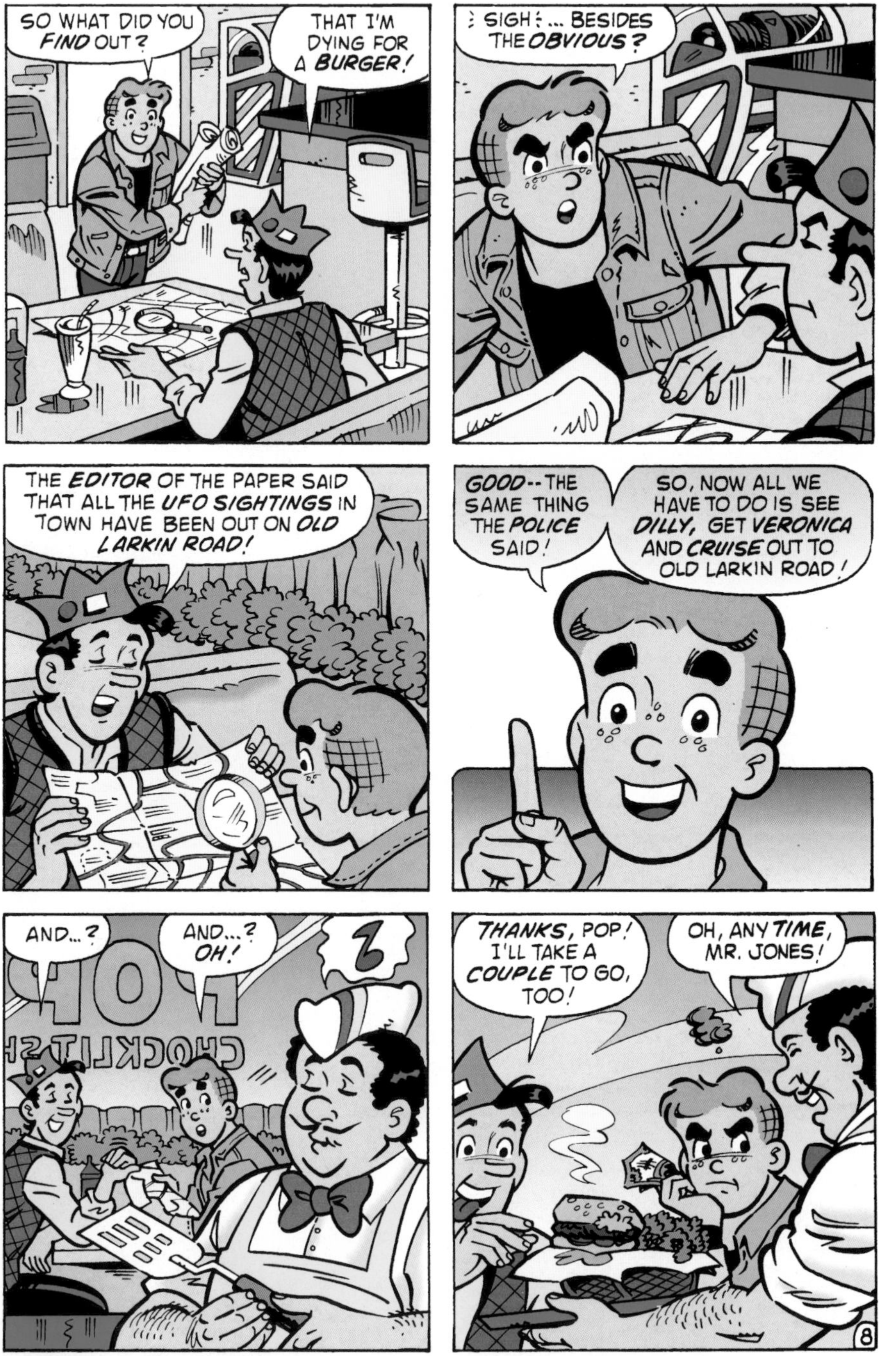
SO WHAT DID YOU FIND OUT?
THAT I'M DYING FOR A BURGER!
: SIGH : ... BESIDES THE OBVIOUS?
THE EDITOR OF THE PAPER SAID THAT ALL THE UFO SIGHTINGS IN TOWN HAVE BEEN OUT ON OLD LARKIN ROAD!
GOOD -- THE SAME THING THE POLICE SAID!
SO, NOW ALL WE HAVE TO DO IS SEE DILLY, GET VERONICA AND CRUISE OUT TO OLD LARKIN ROAD!
AND...?
AND...? OH!
POP
CHOCKLIT SH
THANKS, POP! I'LL TAKE A COUPLE TO GO, TOO!
OH, ANY TIME, MR. JONES!
8

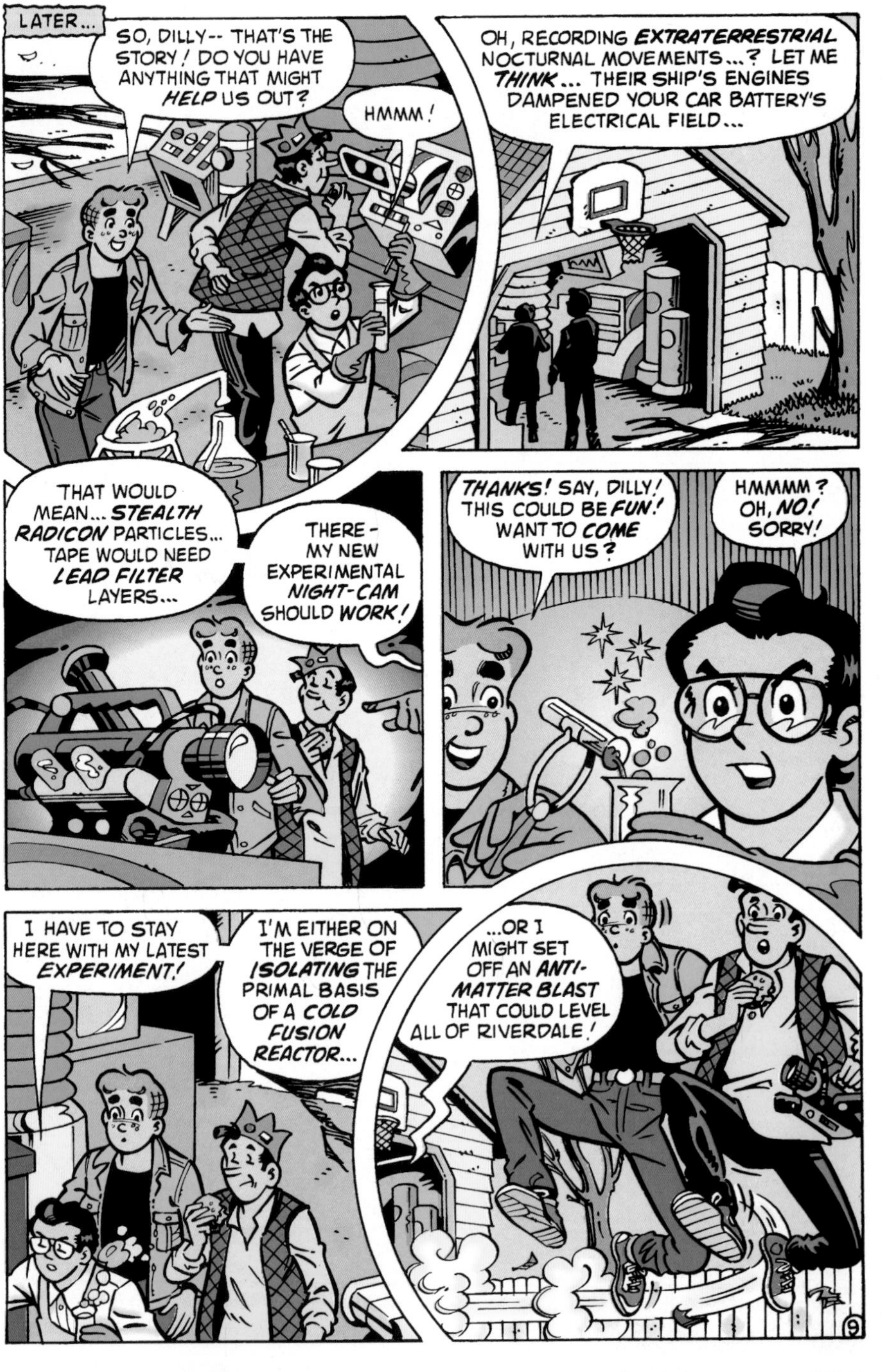
LATER...
SO, DILLY-- THAT'S THE STORY! DO YOU HAVE ANYTHING THAT MIGHT HELP US OUT?
HMMM!
OH, RECORDING EXTRATERRESTRIAL NOCTURNAL MOVEMENTS...? LET ME THINK... THEIR SHIP'S ENGINES DAMPENED YOUR CAR BATTERY'S ELECTRICAL FIELD...
THAT WOULD MEAN... STEALTH RADICON PARTICLES... TAPE WOULD NEED LEAD FILTER LAYERS...
THERE - MY NEW EXPERIMENTAL NIGHT-CAM SHOULD WORK!
THANKS! SAY, DILLY! THIS COULD BE FUN! WANT TO COME WITH US?
HMMMM? OH, NO! SORRY!
I HAVE TO STAY HERE WITH MY LATEST EXPERIMENT!
I'M EITHER ON THE VERGE OF ISOLATING THE PRIMAL BASIS OF A COLD FUSION REACTOR...
...OR I MIGHT SET OFF AN ANTI-MATTER BLAST THAT COULD LEVEL ALL OF RIVERDALE!
9

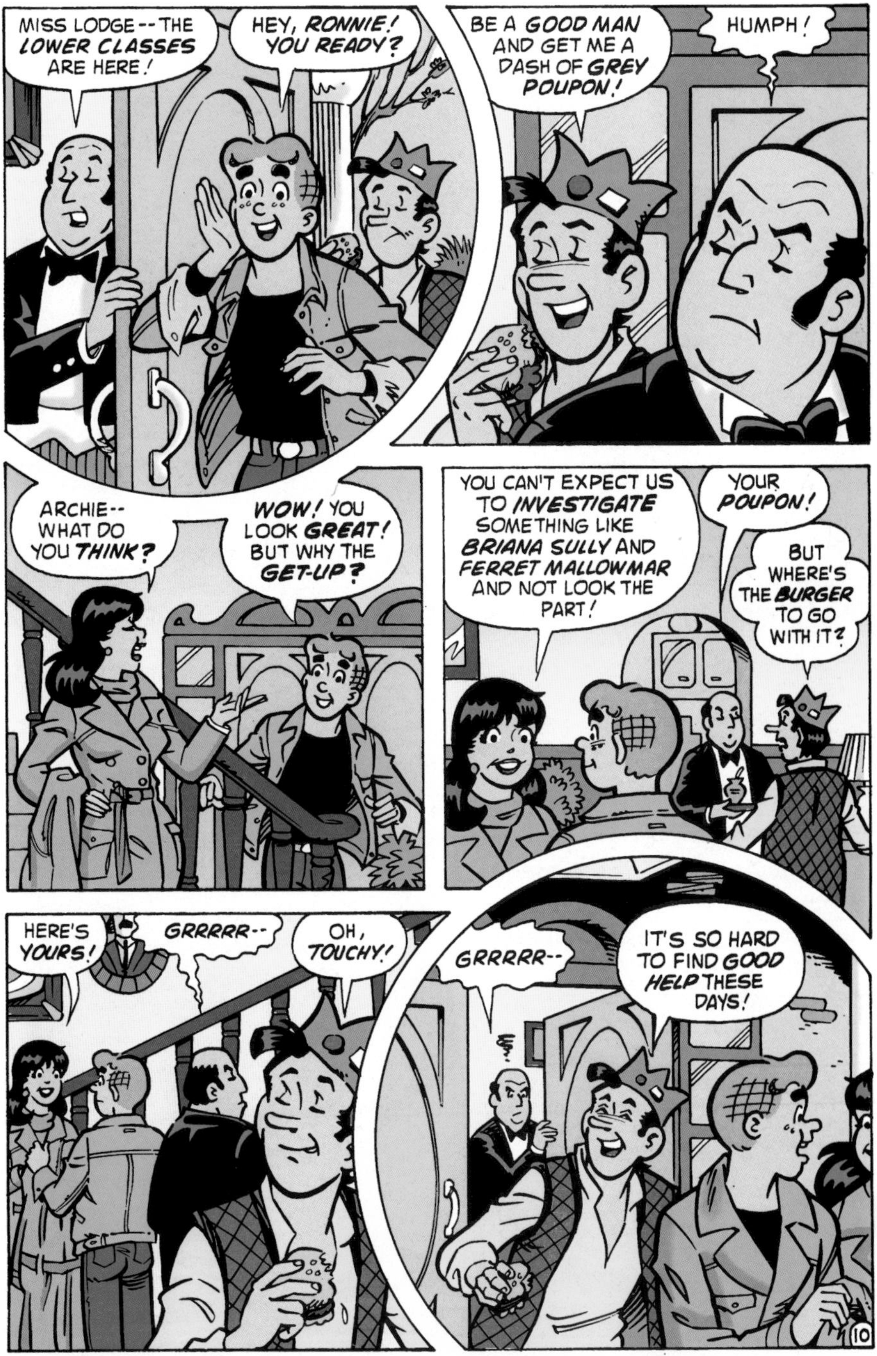
MISS LODGE -- THE LOWER CLASSES ARE HERE!
HEY, RONNIE! YOU READY?
BE A GOOD MAN AND GET ME A DASH OF GREY POUPON!
HUMPH!
ARCHIE-- WHAT DO YOU THINK?
WOW! YOU LOOK GREAT! BUT WHY THE GET-UP?
YOU CAN'T EXPECT US TO INVESTIGATE SOMETHING LIKE BRIANA SULLY AND FERRET MALLOWMAR AND NOT LOOK THE PART!
YOUR POUPON!
BUT WHERE'S THE BURGER TO GO WITH IT?
HERE'S YOURS!
GRRRRR--
OH, TOUCHY!
GRRRRR--
IT'S SO HARD TO FIND GOOD HELP THESE DAYS!
10

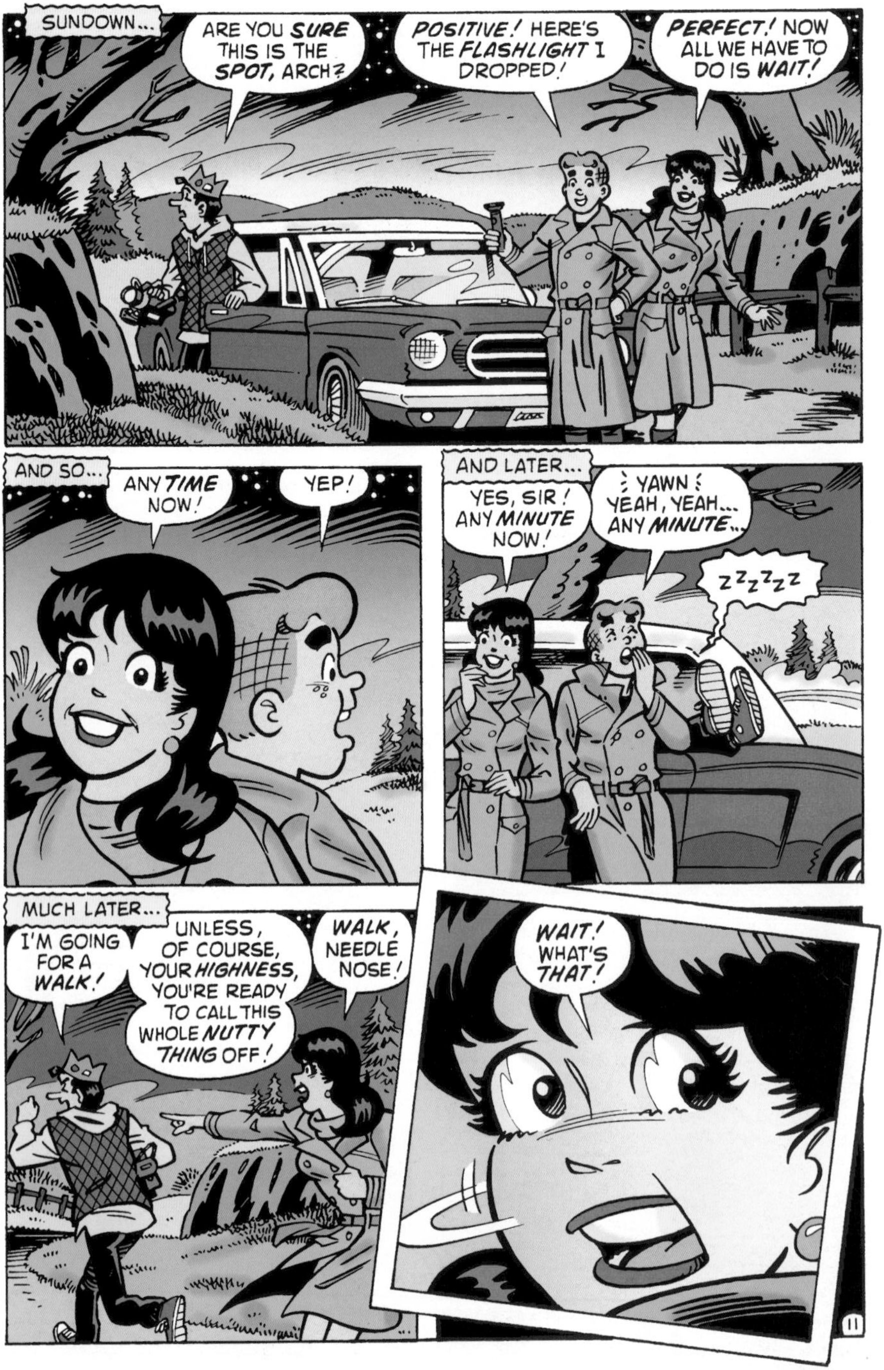
SUNDOWN...
ARE YOU SURE THIS IS THE SPOT, ARCH?
POSITIVE! HERE'S THE FLASHLIGHT I DROPPED!
PERFECT! NOW ALL WE HAVE TO DO IS WAIT!
AND SO...
ANY TIME NOW!
YEP!
AND LATER...
YES, SIR! ANY MINUTE NOW!
YAWN YEAH, YEAH... ANY MINUTE...
ZZZZZZ
MUCH LATER...
I'M GOING FOR A WALK!
UNLESS, OF COURSE, YOUR HIGHNESS, YOU'RE READY TO CALL THIS WHOLE NUTTY THING OFF!
WALK, NEEDLE NOSE!
WAIT! WHAT'S THAT!
11

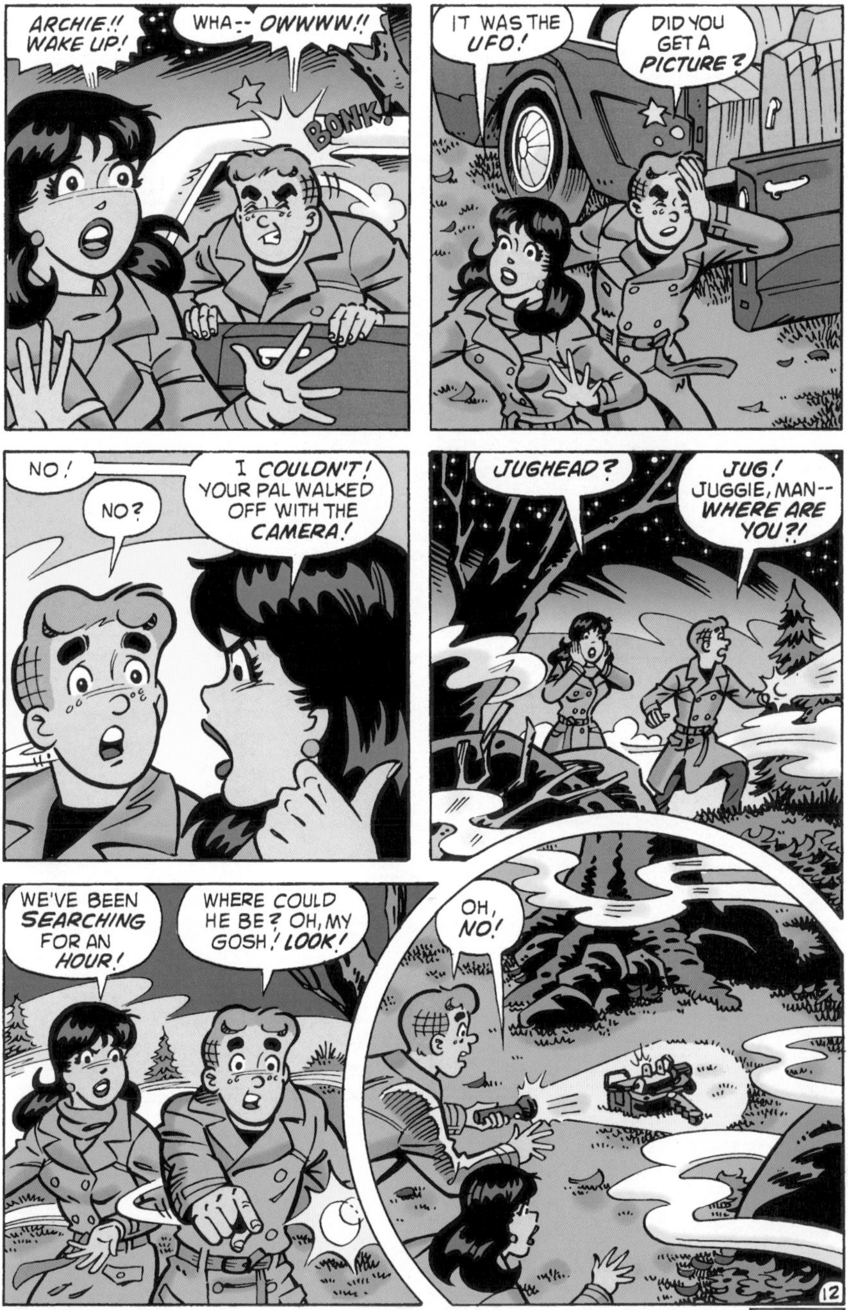
ARCHIE!! WAKE UP!
WHA-- OWWWW!!
BONK!
IT WAS THE UFO!
DID YOU GET A PICTURE?
NO!
NO?
I COULDN'T! YOUR PAL WALKED OFF WITH THE CAMERA!
JUGHEAD?
JUG! JUGGIE, MAN-- WHERE ARE YOU?!
WE'VE BEEN SEARCHING FOR AN HOUR!
WHERE COULD HE BE? OH, MY GOSH! LOOK!
OH, NO!
12
CONTINUED

Archie X-FOLDERS! PART III

WOW! WHAT *HAPPENED* TO ME?

OH, MAN! I'M ON AN ALIEN *SHIP!*

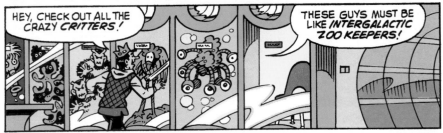

HEY, CHECK OUT ALL THE CRAZY *CRITTERS!*

THESE GUYS MUST BE LIKE *INTERGALACTIC ZOO KEEPERS!*

HUH! *WONDER* WHAT THEY PLAN ON *PUTTING* IN THIS ONE?

GULP

EARTH SPECIMEN!

13

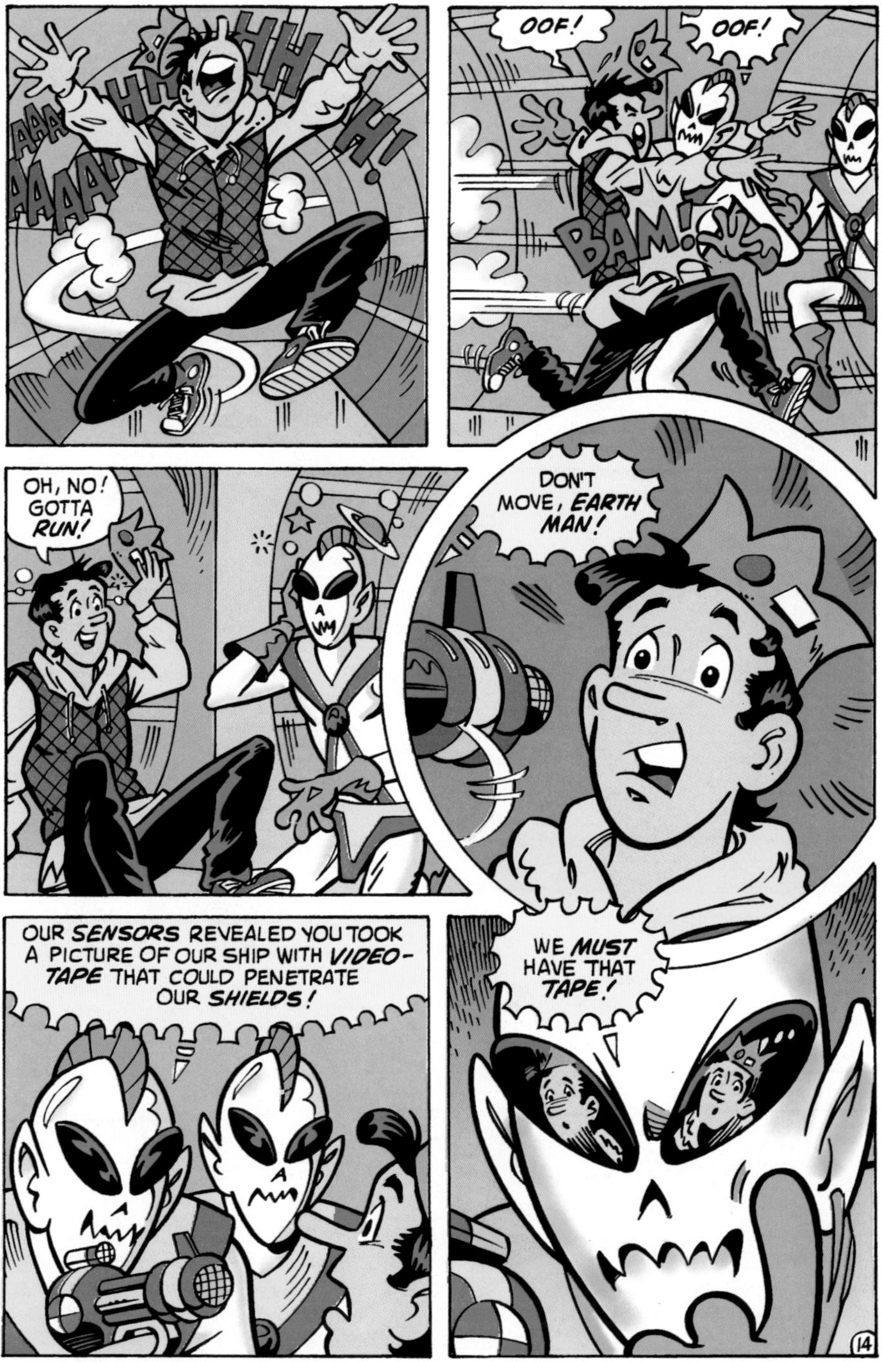
AAAAAHHHHHHH!
OOF!
OOF!
BAM!
OH, NO! GOTTA RUN!
DON'T MOVE, EARTH MAN!
OUR SENSORS REVEALED YOU TOOK A PICTURE OF OUR SHIP WITH VIDEO-TAPE THAT COULD PENETRATE OUR SHIELDS!
WE MUST HAVE THAT TAPE!
14

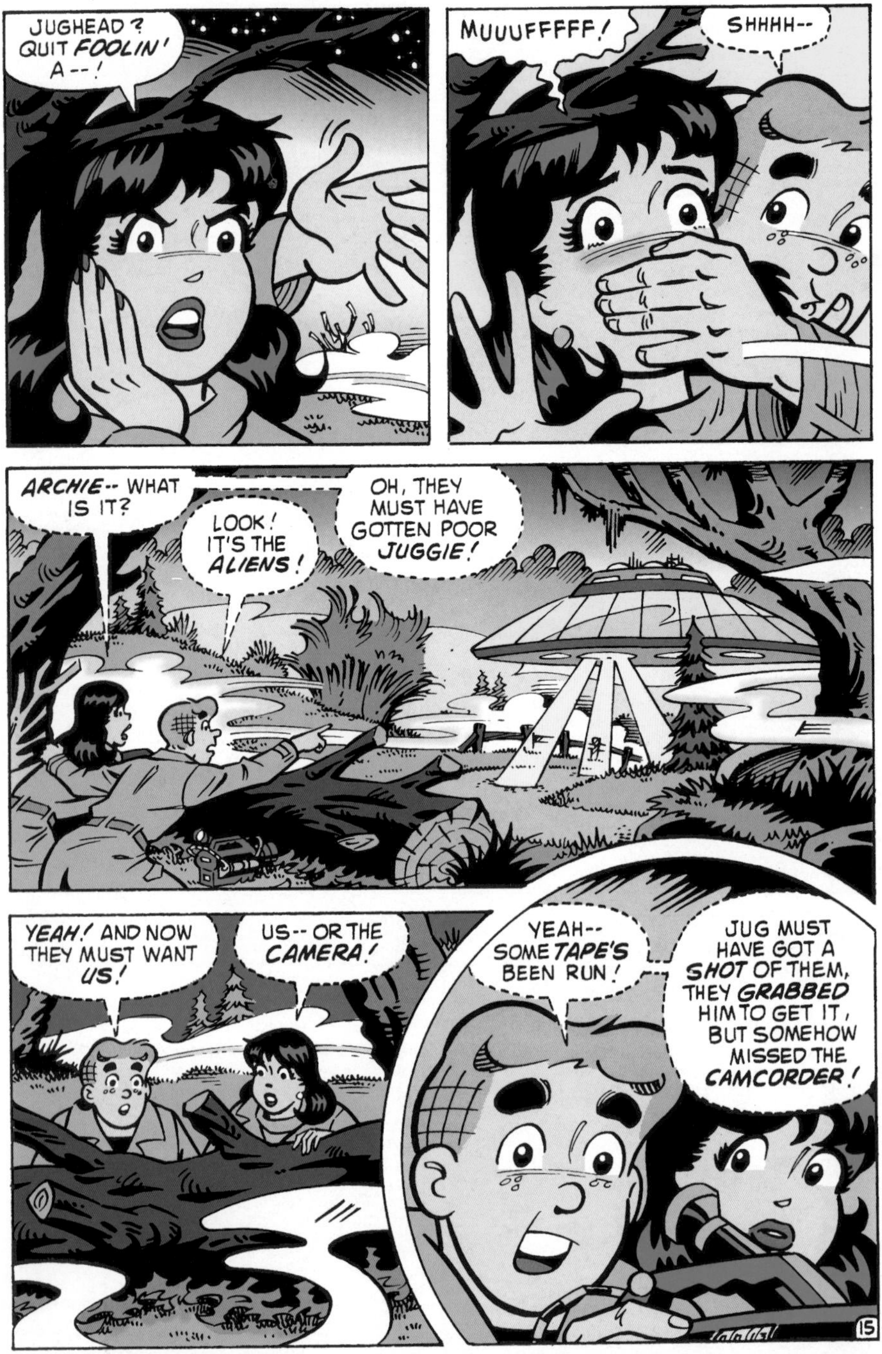
JUGHEAD? QUIT FOOLIN' A--!
MUUUFFFFF!
SHHHH--
ARCHIE-- WHAT IS IT?
LOOK! IT'S THE ALIENS!
OH, THEY MUST HAVE GOTTEN POOR JUGGIE!
YEAH! AND NOW THEY MUST WANT US!
US-- OR THE CAMERA!
YEAH-- SOME TAPE'S BEEN RUN!
JUG MUST HAVE GOT A SHOT OF THEM, THEY GRABBED HIM TO GET IT, BUT SOMEHOW MISSED THE CAMCORDER!
15

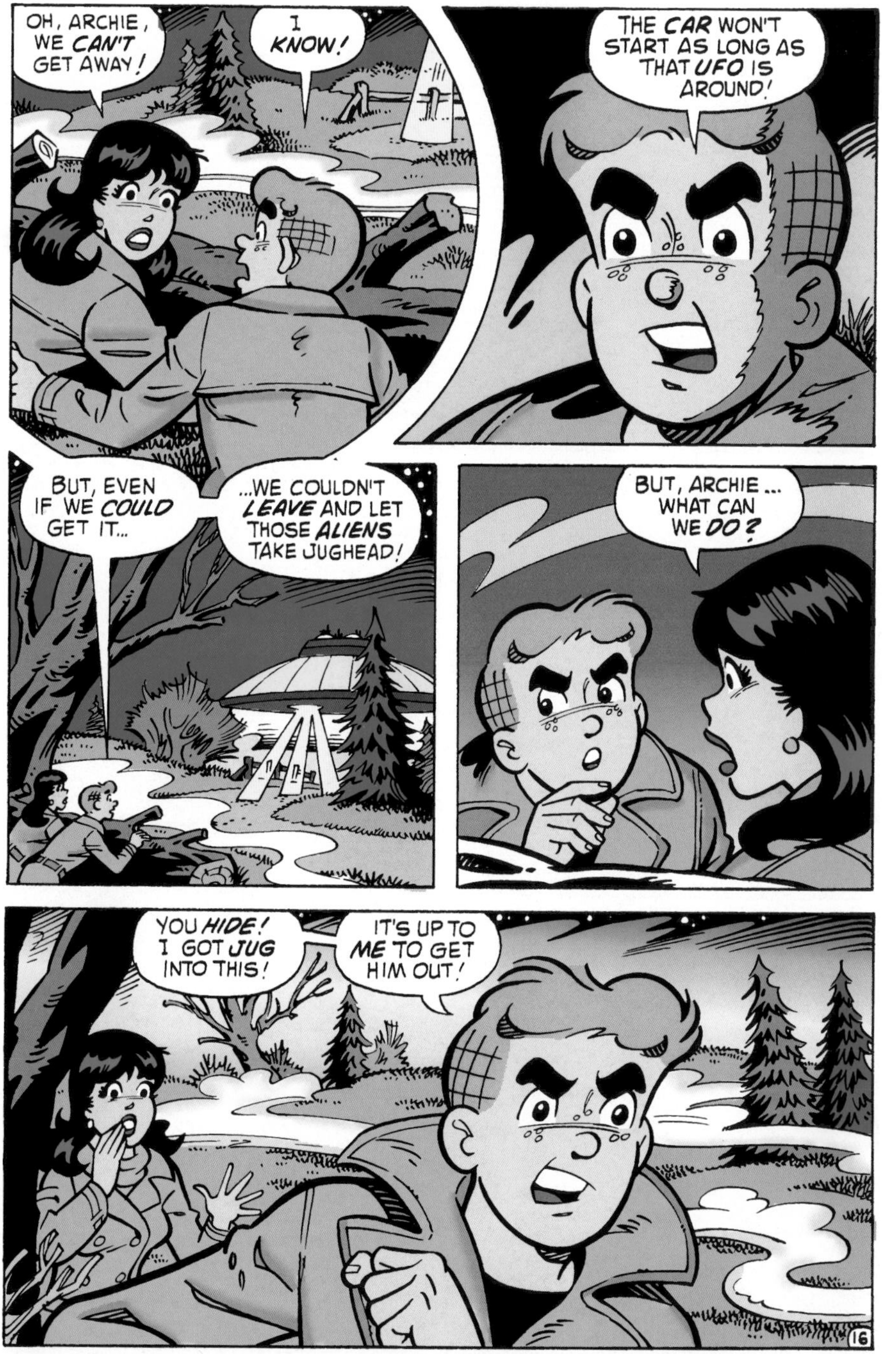
OH, ARCHIE, WE CAN'T GET AWAY!
I KNOW!
THE CAR WON'T START AS LONG AS THAT UFO IS AROUND!
BUT, EVEN IF WE COULD GET IT...
...WE COULDN'T LEAVE AND LET THOSE ALIENS TAKE JUGHEAD!
BUT, ARCHIE ... WHAT CAN WE DO?
YOU HIDE! I GOT JUG INTO THIS!
IT'S UP TO ME TO GET HIM OUT!
16

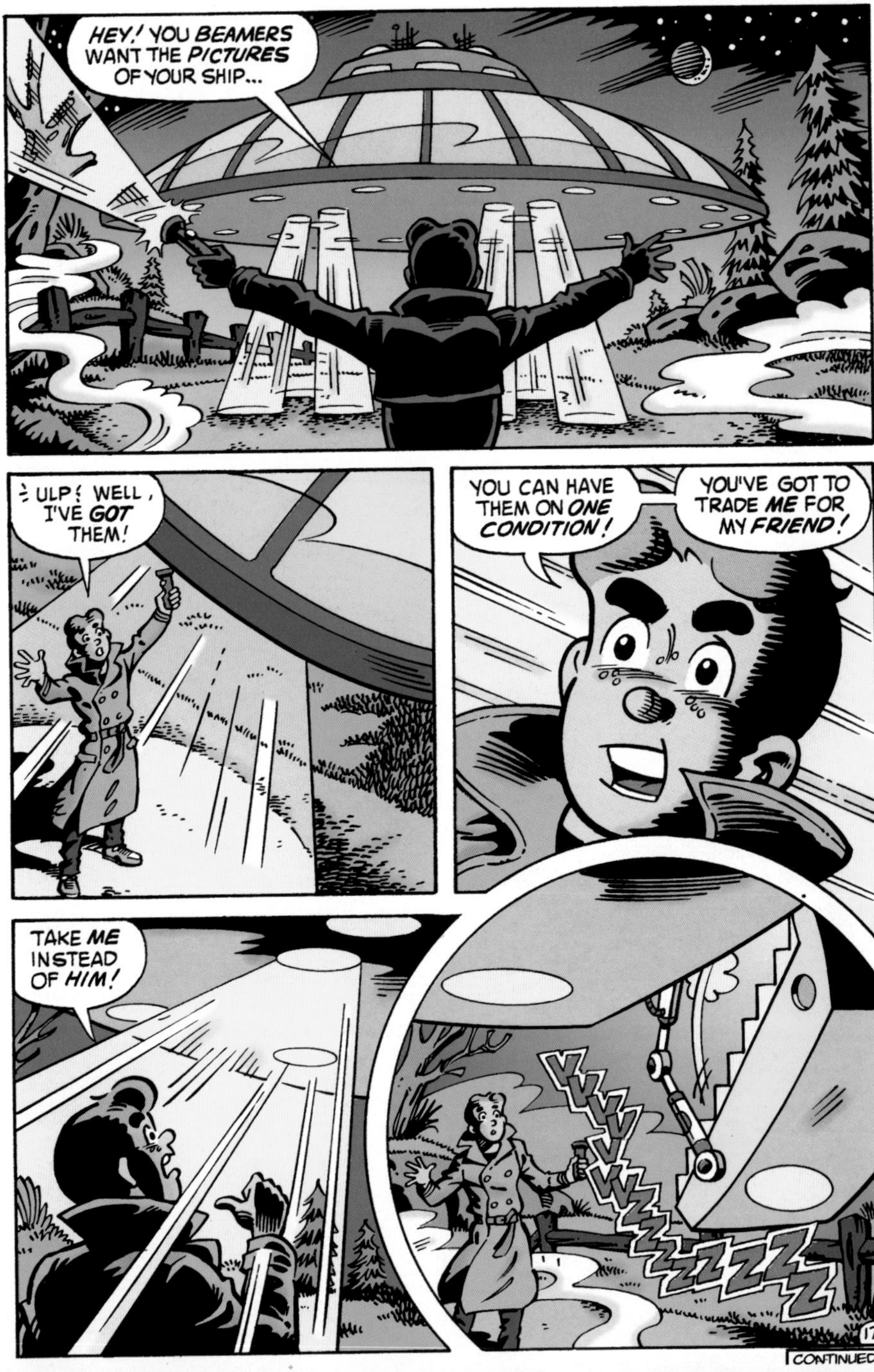
HEY! YOU BEAMERS WANT THE PICTURES OF YOUR SHIP...
ULP! WELL, I'VE GOT THEM!
YOU CAN HAVE THEM ON ONE CONDITION!
YOU'VE GOT TO TRADE ME FOR MY FRIEND!
TAKE ME INSTEAD OF HIM!
VVVVVVVZZZZZZZ
17
CONTINUED

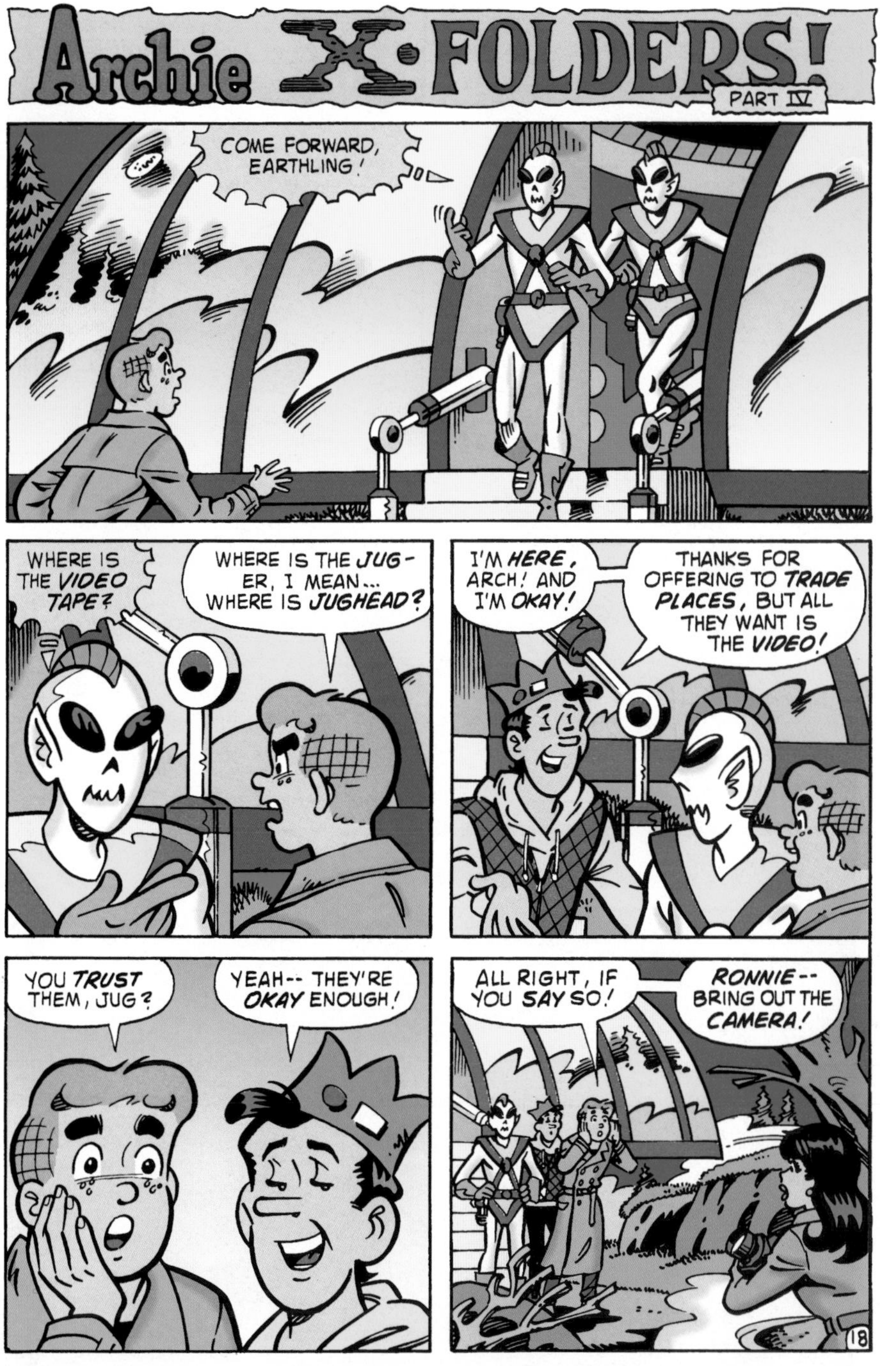
Archie X-FOLDERS!
PART IV
COME FORWARD, EARTHLING!
WHERE IS THE VIDEO TAPE?
WHERE IS THE JUG- ER, I MEAN... WHERE IS JUGHEAD?
I'M HERE, ARCH! AND I'M OKAY!
THANKS FOR OFFERING TO TRADE PLACES, BUT ALL THEY WANT IS THE VIDEO!
YOU TRUST THEM, JUG?
YEAH-- THEY'RE OKAY ENOUGH!
ALL RIGHT, IF YOU SAY SO!
RONNIE-- BRING OUT THE CAMERA!
18

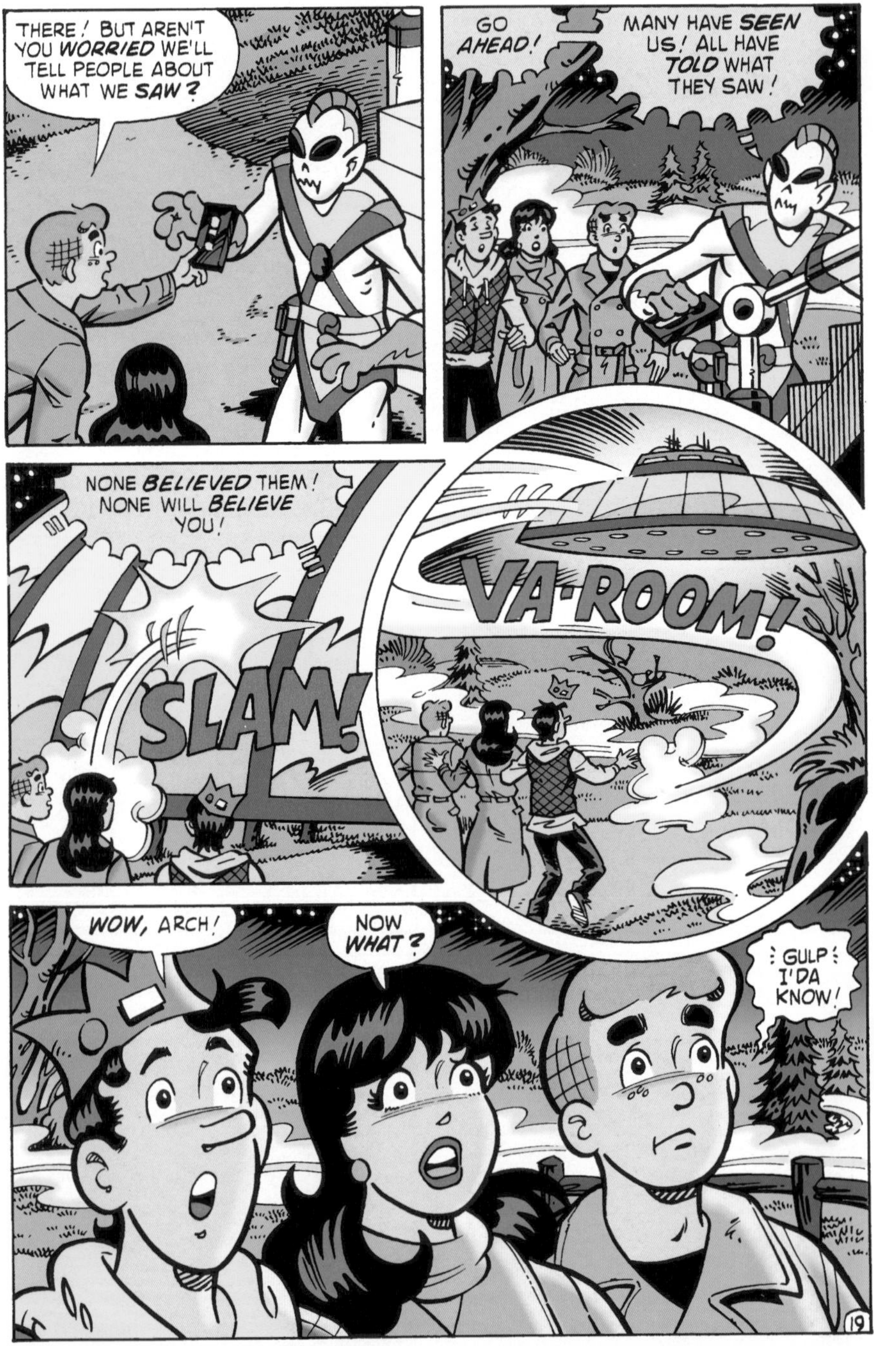
THERE! BUT AREN'T YOU WORRIED WE'LL TELL PEOPLE ABOUT WHAT WE SAW?
GO AHEAD!
MANY HAVE SEEN US! ALL HAVE TOLD WHAT THEY SAW!
NONE BELIEVED THEM! NONE WILL BELIEVE YOU!
SLAM!
VA-ROOM!
WOW, ARCH!
NOW WHAT?
GULP I'DA KNOW!
19

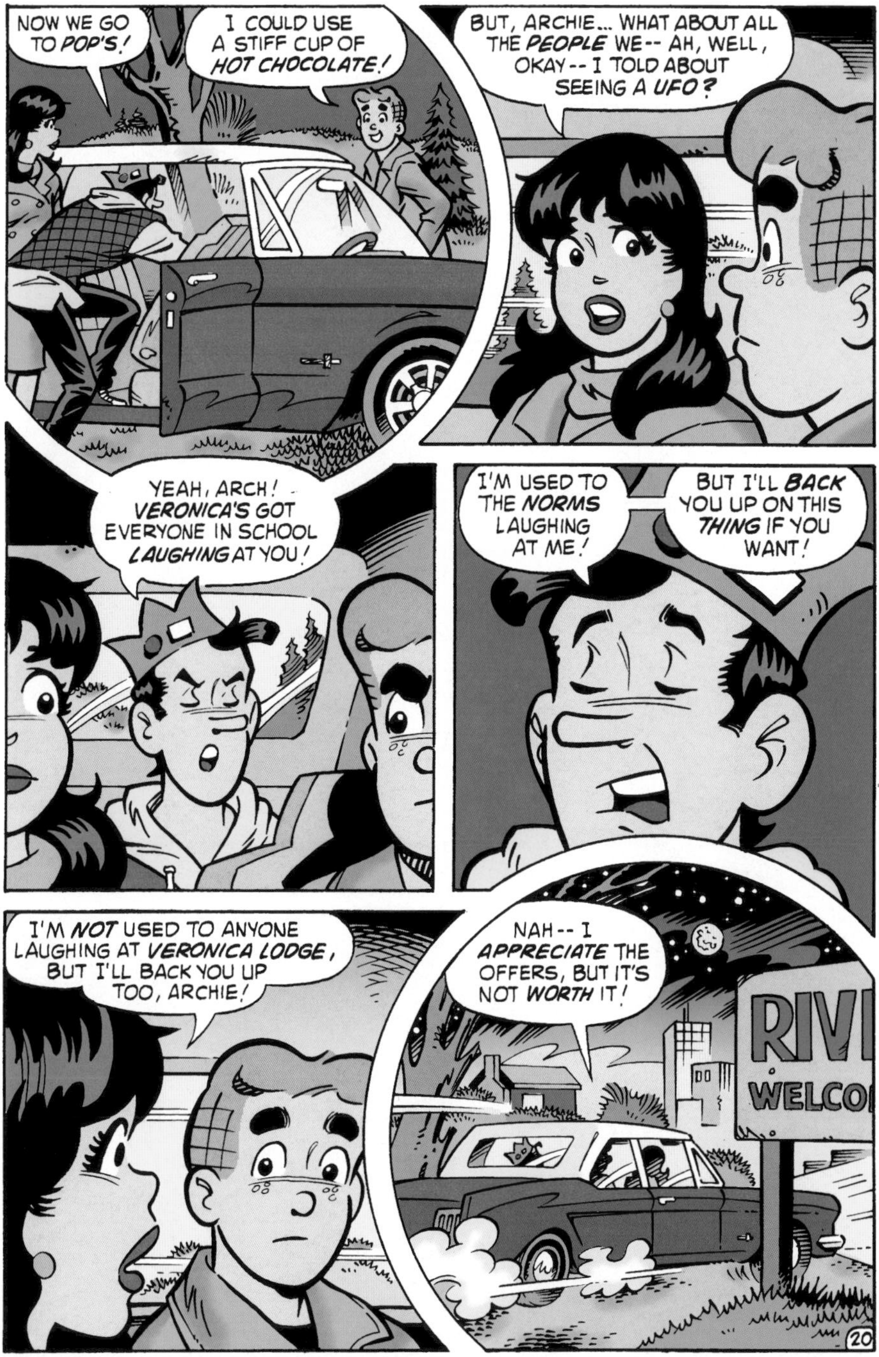
NOW WE GO TO *POP'S*!
I COULD USE A STIFF CUP OF *HOT CHOCOLATE*!
BUT, ARCHIE... WHAT ABOUT ALL THE *PEOPLE* WE-- AH, WELL, OKAY-- I TOLD ABOUT SEEING A *UFO*?
YEAH, ARCH! *VERONICA'S* GOT EVERYONE IN SCHOOL *LAUGHING* AT YOU!
I'M USED TO THE *NORMS* LAUGHING AT ME!
BUT I'LL *BACK* YOU UP ON THIS *THING* IF YOU WANT!
I'M *NOT* USED TO ANYONE LAUGHING AT *VERONICA LODGE*, BUT I'LL BACK YOU UP TOO, ARCHIE!
NAH-- I *APPRECIATE* THE OFFERS, BUT IT'S NOT *WORTH* IT!
RIV
WELCO
20

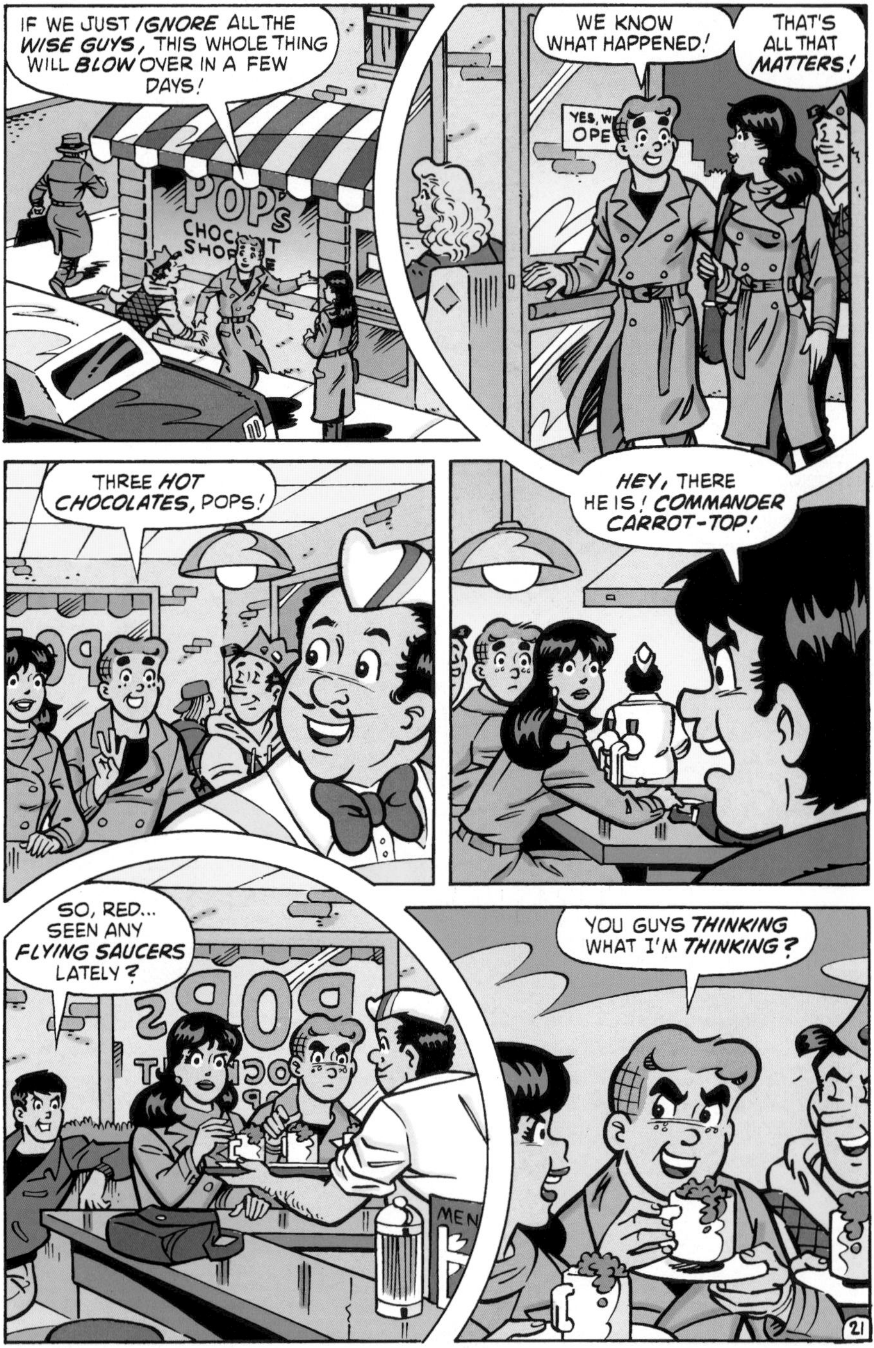
IF WE JUST IGNORE ALL THE WISE GUYS, THIS WHOLE THING WILL BLOW OVER IN A FEW DAYS!
POP'S CHOC SHOP
WE KNOW WHAT HAPPENED!
THAT'S ALL THAT MATTERS!
THREE HOT CHOCOLATES, POPS!
HEY, THERE HE IS! COMMANDER CARROT-TOP!
SO, RED... SEEN ANY FLYING SAUCERS LATELY?
YOU GUYS THINKING WHAT I'M THINKING?
21

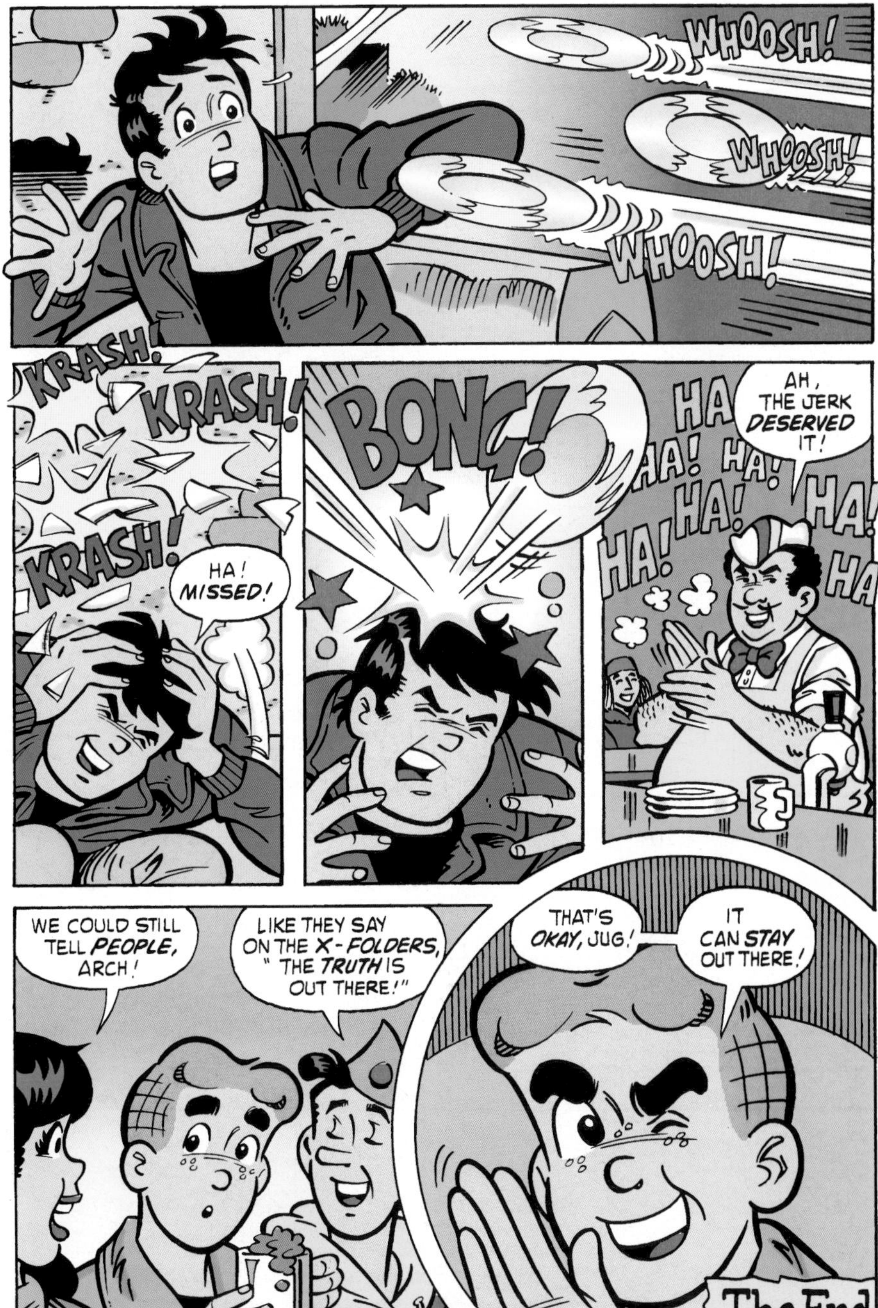
WHOOSH!
WHOOSH!
WHOOSH!
KRASH!
KRASH!
KRASH!
HA! MISSED!
BONG!
HA HA! HA! HA! HA! HA! HA! HA
AH, THE JERK DESERVED IT!
WE COULD STILL TELL PEOPLE, ARCH!
LIKE THEY SAY ON THE X-FOLDERS, " THE TRUTH IS OUT THERE!"
THAT'S OKAY, JUG!
IT CAN STAY OUT THERE!
The End

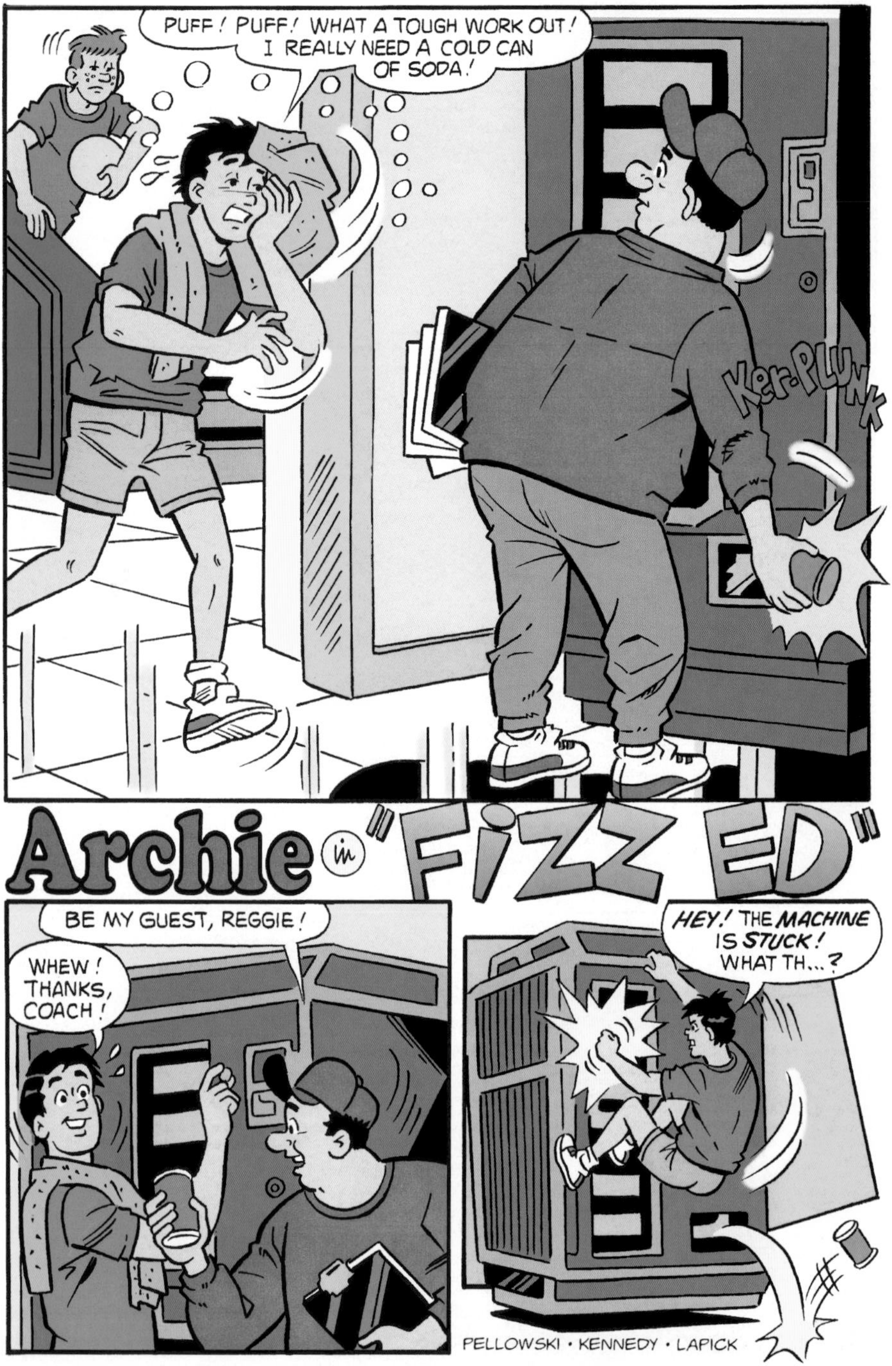
PUFF! PUFF! WHAT A TOUGH WORK OUT! I REALLY NEED A COLD CAN OF SODA!
KER-PLUNK
Archie in "FIZZ ED"
BE MY GUEST, REGGIE!
WHEW! THANKS, COACH!
HEY! THE MACHINE IS STUCK! WHAT TH...?
PELLOWSKI • KENNEDY • LAPICK

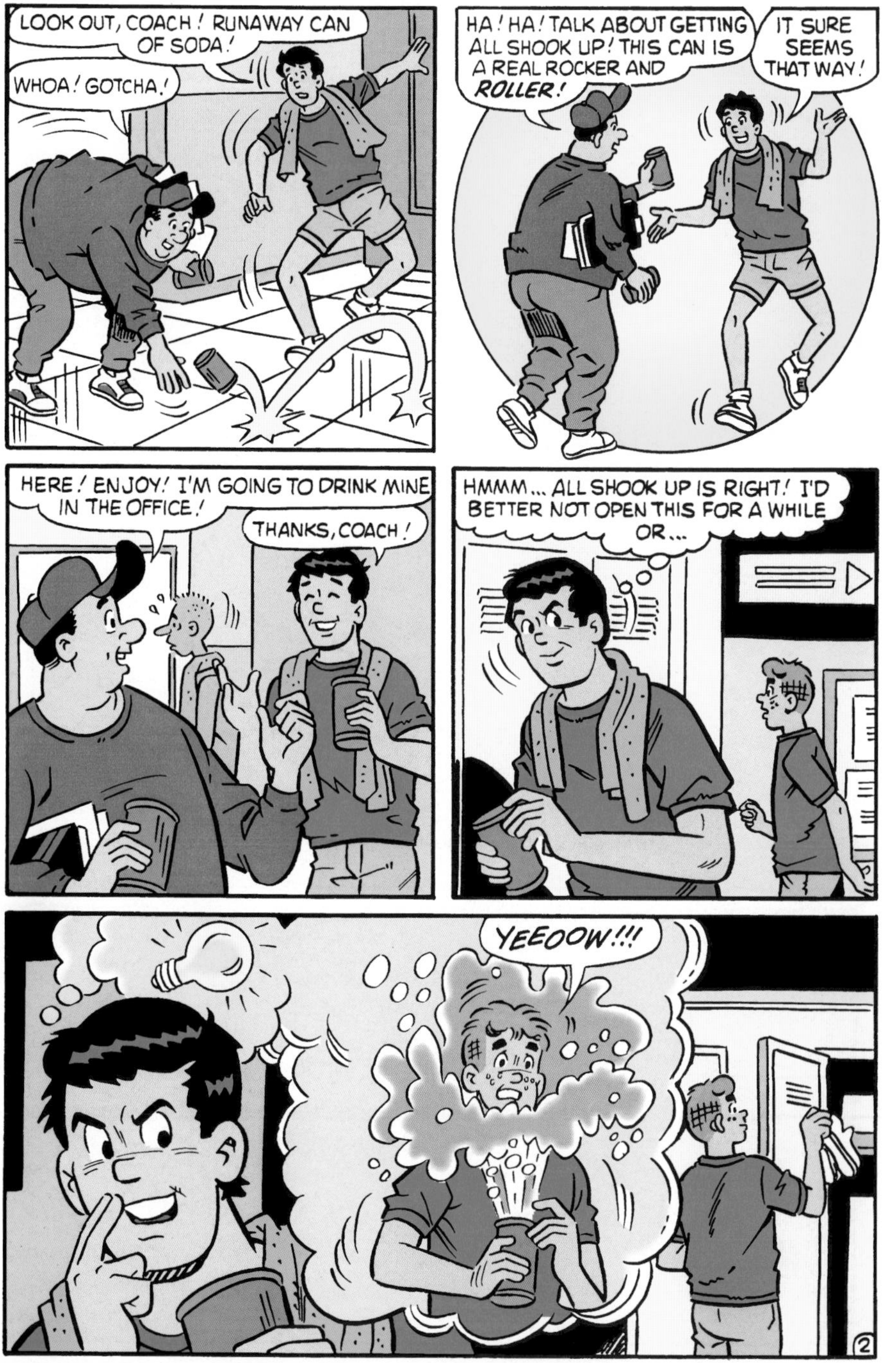
LOOK OUT, COACH! RUNAWAY CAN OF SODA!
WHOA! GOTCHA!
HA! HA! TALK ABOUT GETTING ALL SHOOK UP! THIS CAN IS A REAL ROCKER AND ROLLER!
IT SURE SEEMS THAT WAY!
HERE! ENJOY! I'M GOING TO DRINK MINE IN THE OFFICE!
THANKS, COACH!
HMMM... ALL SHOOK UP IS RIGHT! I'D BETTER NOT OPEN THIS FOR A WHILE OR...
YEEOOW!!!
2

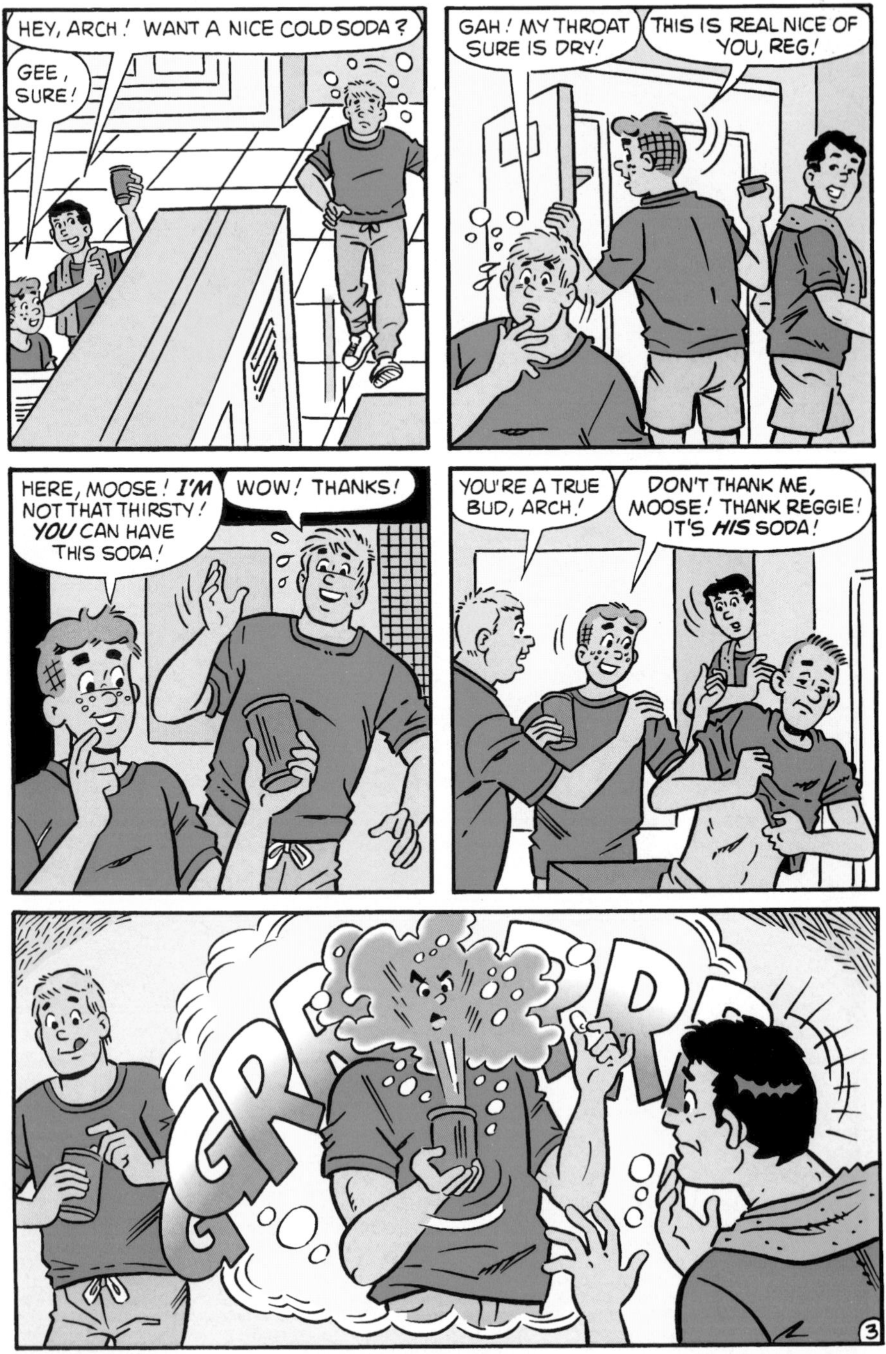
HEY, ARCH! WANT A NICE COLD SODA?
GEE, SURE!
GAH! MY THROAT SURE IS DRY!
THIS IS REAL NICE OF YOU, REG!
HERE, MOOSE! *I'M* NOT THAT THIRSTY! *YOU* CAN HAVE THIS SODA!
WOW! THANKS!
YOU'RE A TRUE BUD, ARCH!
DON'T THANK ME, MOOSE! THANK REGGIE! IT'S *HIS* SODA!

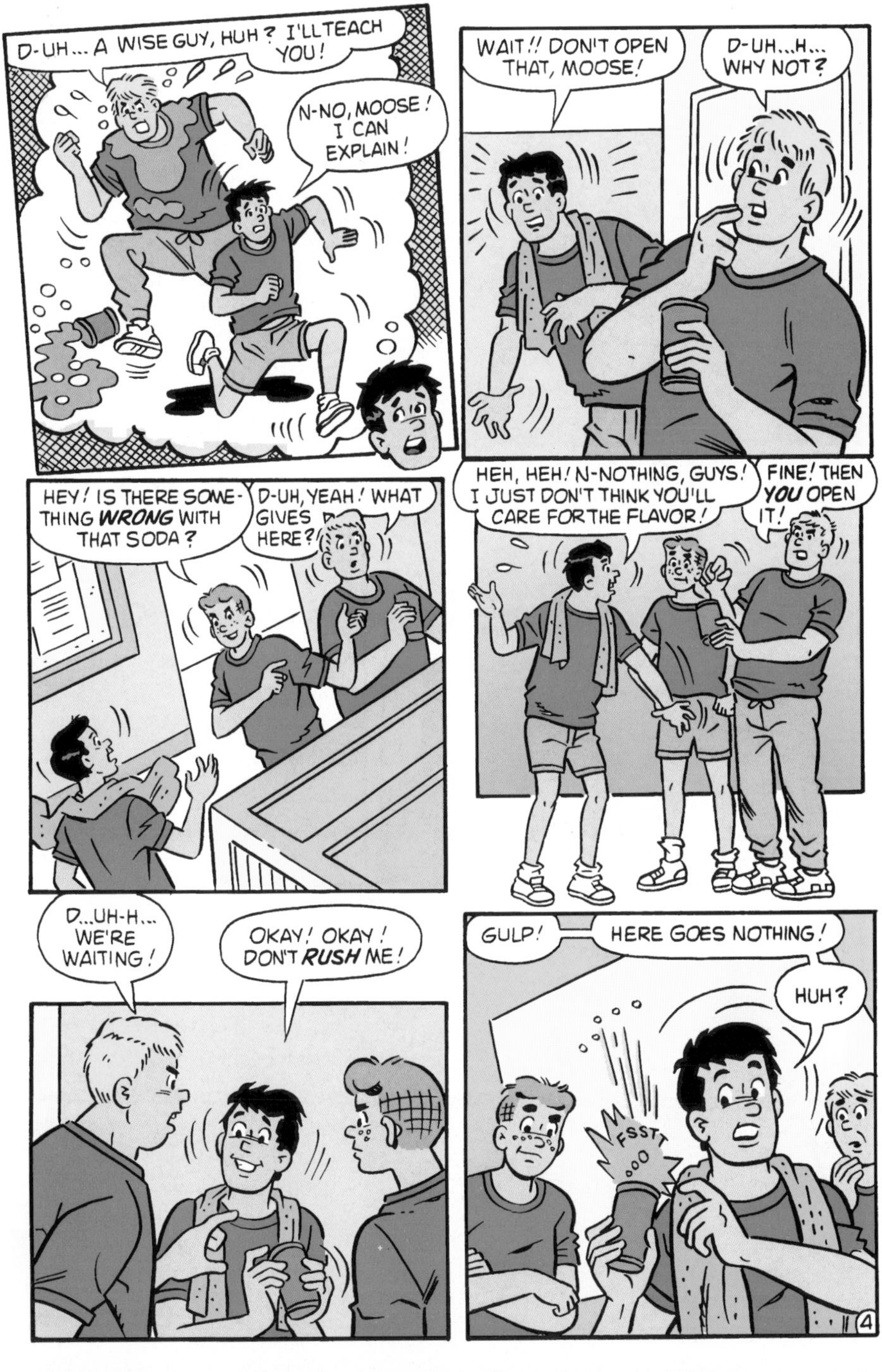
D-UH... A WISE GUY, HUH? I'LL TEACH YOU!
N-NO, MOOSE! I CAN EXPLAIN!
WAIT!! DON'T OPEN THAT, MOOSE!
D-UH...H... WHY NOT?
HEY! IS THERE SOMETHING WRONG WITH THAT SODA?
D-UH, YEAH! WHAT GIVES HERE?
HEH, HEH! N-NOTHING, GUYS! I JUST DON'T THINK YOU'LL CARE FOR THE FLAVOR!
FINE! THEN YOU OPEN IT!
D...UH-H... WE'RE WAITING!
OKAY! OKAY! DON'T RUSH ME!
GULP!
HERE GOES NOTHING!
HUH?
FSSTT
4

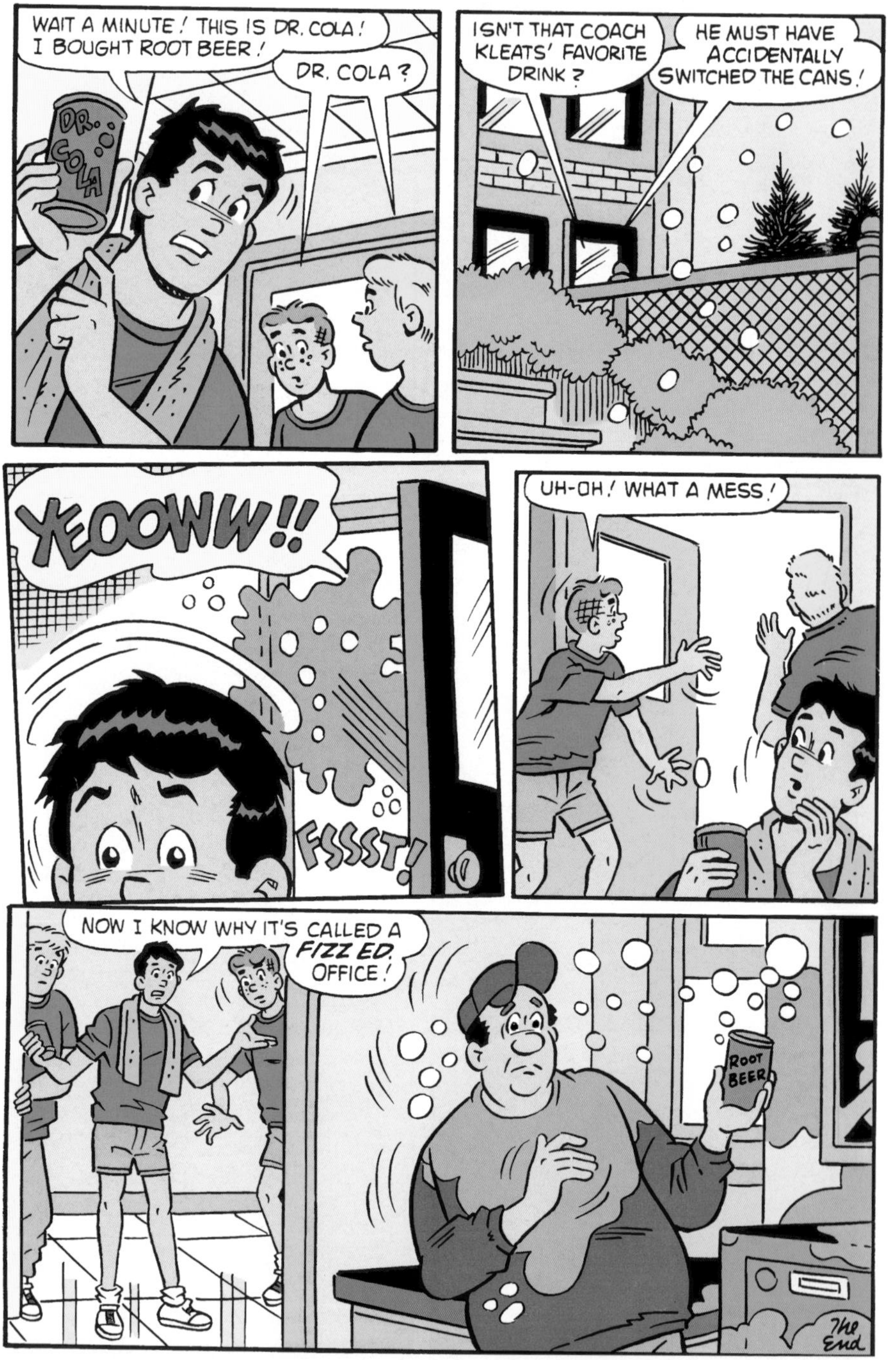
WAIT A MINUTE! THIS IS DR. COLA! I BOUGHT ROOT BEER!
DR. COLA?
DR. COLA
ISN'T THAT COACH KLEATS' FAVORITE DRINK?
HE MUST HAVE ACCIDENTALLY SWITCHED THE CANS!
YEOOWW!!
FSSST!
UH-OH! WHAT A MESS!
NOW I KNOW WHY IT'S CALLED A *FIZZ ED.* OFFICE!
ROOT BEER
The End